System of Trees

Liam Adams

Cover illustration by Liam Adams

**System of Trees**

by Liam Adams

everyoneneedsaliam.com.au

We think this book is mostly suited to young adults, 10-12 and over, although older adults may enjoy it as much!

This book is copyright and may not be reproduced in any manner without consulting the author. All intellectual property including cover artwork belongs to the author.

This book is sold on the understanding that it is the work of a person with intellectual disability and Autism. All creativity is from the author and the text has been edited by his mother to the best of her ability. However, it is understood that the writing may be different from that expected in a formally published novel.

Liam hopes you enjoy reading his book as much as he enjoyed writing it. He would love to hear your feedback; if you wish to contact him his email address is ltahm@icloud.com

Canberra, Australia, October 2023

ISBN: 978- 0-6455970-3-5

Table of Contents

Foreword

Breaking Barriers, Shaping Minds: How Liam's Work Inspires Change

As I reflect upon Liam's latest remarkable book, I continue to be in awe of his incredible spirit which shines through every word. I am reminded of the immense power of human resilience and the ability to obliterate the barriers that life continues to throw at us as we proceed through our lives. Liam's journey is nothing short of extraordinary, for he has not only overcome many of the challenges of autism and intellectual disability but has also harnessed his unique perspective to create yet another work that is equal parts engaging, educational and hilarious.

In a world that often struggles to understand and accommodate the diverse needs of people with disability and other life challenges, Liam's voice emerges as a source of great strength and inspiration. His work and his capacity for growth are of great significance, not only within our community at the Network but also within the hearts of countless individuals who face similar hurdles. With each sentence carefully crafted, Liam invites us to witness his incredible mind for storytelling in science fiction.

I have had the pleasure of getting to know Liam since he was in his mid-teens. A major component of his brilliance stems from his unbeatable sense of humour. It is a delightful gift that permeates each page of his books, infusing them with a unique charm and levity. Liam's wit and cleverness are clear in the way he intertwines imaginative worlds with playful banter and unexpected twists. His words have the power to transport us to distant galaxies while simultaneously bringing a smile to our faces. Through his storytelling, Liam reminds us that even in the face of adversity, laughter can be a source of strength and joy. His infectious humour serves as a testament to his resilient spirit and his ability to find lightness amidst the challenges he has faced. With every turn of the page, we are reminded of the power of laughter and the beauty of finding joy in unexpected places.

As the CEO of the Network, an organisation dedicated to advocating for the rights and wellbeing of people with mental health issues, it is both an honour and a privilege to support Liam on his journey. Through a small business grant, we hope to provide him with the means to further his literary pursuits and reach an even wider audience. Liam's work holds great significance for our community, as it not only challenges preconceived notions and stereotypes but also offers encouragement to others facing their own unique battles.

Personally, Liam's unwavering persistence to his career strikes a deep chord within me. Coming from a family with many disabilities and other life challenges, including my own, I understand firsthand the importance of representation and the power of storytelling. Liam's journey reminds me that our struggles need not define us; rather, they can become the very fuel that propels us forward on our journey towards self-discovery.

Through this foreword, I urge every reader, whether they face disability, other life challenges, or simply the universal human experience, to embrace the extraordinary. Liam's journey exemplifies the resilience of the human spirit and is a reminder that we are all valuable; we all matter. We just need to be given a chance and have the strength to take it. It is through supporting the endeavours of the world's Liams that we create a more inclusive and compassionate world.

In a world hungry for authenticity and brimming with untold stories, it is clear that, no matter what we have in this life... Everyone Needs A Liam.

Dalane Drexler
Chief Executive Officer
ACT Mental Health Consumer Network Inc.

Preface

"You gotta love nature, don't ya?"

"Yes, I don't have any problem with nature at all. Except when it tries to kill you, eat you, or strangle you to death".

Liam Adams, System of Trees

The idea started with Spring, plants, a park, and a wedding.

It all came around just when I was about to begin the Librarian Saga series. I took a lot of notes and brainstormed about what these books would be all about, as all of them are stories on their own.

Papers Through the Hollows was the start of the series, at the end of which the main character, Floyd decided to enter into a universe he thought was worth exploring. This was followed by *The Lost Humans*, where we see Floyd actually set off into the cosmos.

System of Trees, however, is the first one in the series where you get the taste that it has no tie to the first two, which you can read totally independently. *System of Trees* is also the first one in the series where we are introduced to one of Floyd's newest friends, Charlotte! Besides Ryan (*The Lost Humans*), this was another character I wanted to bring into the Librarian Saga cast. And there is a big difference between Ryan and Charlotte. (If you intend to read *The Lost Humans*, I will keep it spoiler-free). Ryan lives on a space station, somewhere across the cosmos in the far future; while Charlotte, on the other hand, lives on Earth in 2012.

She isn't the only character in the series Floyd encountered that lived on Earth. On Floyd's first adventure, he stumbled across two teenagers, Jack and Vicky, in the year 2016. With Charlotte, I thought I wanted to bring her excitement and interest into the book; while Ryan was more just 'on the ride'. Charlotte wanted an adventure to go on, and boy! what an adventure it is!

This is my only book I wrote from someone's point of view, and Charlotte really captures the way she sees everything, both the wonderful and the scary. But Charlotte is only half of this exciting cast.

(I'll leave an intriguing question for you big fans: Ryan and Charlotte are two completely different people in two different time zones. Do you think will we ever see them together on an adventure with our lovable librarian Floyd?)

Looking at the plant and tree features of the book. Why did I write about that? Well, as I briefly mentioned earlier, it was around the time a friend of mine was getting married.

Me and my mum were going to pick up some plants at a plant shop near a garden. I looked at a particular area in the shop which gave me glimpse of an idea on how Charlotte may first meet Floyd. Then I dug deeper.

Lake Burley Griffin – photo by Liam Adams 2023
Inspired the location where the wedding is set.

When I was small, there was a park that had a more glimmer section with bushes all around and four benches on each side.

I felt like that area was perfect for what I wanted for the book. So the *System of Trees* began right there!

The bushy setting with a seat you can just see – Lennox Gardens, Canberra – photo by Liam Adams 2023 Inspired Liam's idea of where Charlotte meets Floyd.

Liam sitting on the bench, as he imagined Floyd, in the bushy garden at Lennox Gardens, Canberra – photo by Jennifer Adams 2023

I knew this book was going to be different as I wanted to bring out the seasoning spirit.

Do you ever feel like in Spring that you're in your zone? That everything seems so calming and wonderful?

That's what I get most of the time every year around in that season; why is that?

Flower from Floriade, Canberra – photo by Liam Adams 2023

Originally, I planned out that Floyd and Charlotte were going to different worlds and planets that had more of a nature base, but it soon came to be an adventure inside a place called "the Bark".

The Bark is wild and bizarre place which might be my strangest world-building I've done so far.

So that's all from me for another exiting story waiting within these pages. Hopefully you'll enjoy reading this novel as much I did writing it!

Liam Adams, Spring 2023

1) An Unwelcome Guest or just Another Stranger

It was around Springtime in 2012, and it was my big sister's wedding. A special day for her. Wearing a white long dress that really suited her. And with the perfect man in her life.

I was happy for her, I mean that. Even though I knew I had nothing to look forward to in my life or anything I could jump into. Life for me wasn't anything but very ordinary.

My name is Charlotte Gore, and this was my very unexpected day that I never imagined would happen.

So, of course, this day was my sister Dorothy's wedding. We were having the ceremony in the city park. We lived in a town nearby, but she wanted her own wedding to be in her favourite park in the city.

I was wearing a simple purple dress with my flat shoes. It wasn't what I wanted, but I came as nice as possible. We were sitting at a row of tables watching my sister and her husband right at the front of the river. I, of course, was sitting with my brother Dale, his wife and their two sons. They got married last year.

"Boy, this is some wedding, eh?" Dale commented to me.

"Yes, I haven't seen anything like it," I said.

I wasn't quite myself that day. I felt as though my family had so much going on in their lives; they were happy about their futures, but my future hadn't been thought out clearly yet, even though I was 20. There was just something missing for me. Something I wanted to get into; right then.

Dale looked at Dorothy, "I'm so happy for both of them".

"Both?" I said quite confused but later I realised I was speaking dumbly, "Oh, Dorothy!" I was eating some sort of egg, so I didn't catch the last bit of what my brother said.

Dale leant back and told me, "Hey, don't you worry; I'll bet there will be something for you to look forward to soon enough".

"Yeah," I said, mumbling, "I mean, I'm still looking for it, you know what I mean?"

What could there be? I mean, we lived a simple life. Nothing weird. We didn't even go to the city that often. But I just didn't really know what I wanted.

If you catch my drift: what was there that could grab my attention and show me something wonderful and exciting? That's what I wanted, I thought, and it seemed impossible! I wondered if there was something that would spark my mind, something I wanted to go towards and reach. A goal. That's what I wanted, and I had been searching for it for two years, but nothing had come to mind.

With everyone watching the bride and the groom and chatting among themselves, I felt like I needed to take a walk. To get some fresh air.

Hey, I wasn't totally abandoning my sister's wedding; sometimes you just need to go out and taste the world.

"Hey, you wouldn't mind if I just pop out for a moment?" I asked Dale, "It looks like they're not about to do anything for a while".

"Yeah, sure" Dale told me, as I walked off.

I was in the garden area and passed by some bushes. There were very formal bushes with flowers on both sides of where I was walking. It was quite pretty seeing it in this weather. It was Spring, and I guess it was a perfect time to smell excellent flowers.

After a while, I spotted an odd man. I don't usually say that about anyone, but this guy was especially different. He was sitting on a bench in the centre with very odd clothes. He was wearing a purple robe with slippers and a suit underneath.

I wanted to say 'I rest my case' on why this guy was strange, but that was not the only thing I noticed. He was reading a book that seemed so bizarre that I wanted to know the name of it.

The title was: '*1,500 things you may not know in the universe, and only 50 you know already*'. The cover looked pretty sci-fi, but I noticed that it also seemed realistic, which was very weird. It had an image of the cosmos on the cover, on which I could tell that no one did any digital effects.

I thought I might ask, "Umm, have you seen a waitress with my drink? I was rushing towards her and I think I lost her."

While still reading, the odd man straightened his open arm and pointed in the direction the waitress went. I was quite surprised that there was even one here! I wondered if she got lost.

I know I shouldn't nick-pick into anyone's business, but I was curious about the book he was reading. Why was I so fascinated by this?

I sat next to him and tried to see if I could read a few pages.

"What are you reading?" I asked, as I tried to read a few glimpses of it.

"Something you shouldn't be looking at," he said as he closed the book on me.

I wasn't entirely pleased; I wanted to see what the book was. "Are you part of the wedding guest list?"

"Well, no," he replied, "But I am waiting for someone".

I frowned at him, wondering why he was here. I knew he wasn't part of the wedding because I would know someone who wore such strange clothes.

I looked over at the plants around us, "You gotta love nature, don't ya?"

"Yes, I don't have any problem with nature at all. Except when it tries to kill you, eat you, or strangle you to death".

I turned, "What?" and chuckled.

"No, I mean, it can try to kill you, even while it tries to be very calming. But that's nature!"

I wasn't sure what kind of man I was chatting to, but he did speak about things even stranger than his looks.

"Why did you close that book?" I asked.

He put the book on his lap and shook his arm.

"I cannot tell you for a billion reasons," he said as he tried to be smart (but I didn't think he was).

"Like what?" I asked him curiously.

He glared, then spoke, "Because I cannot tell you about what may happen in the future. I can't give away spoilers from movies that haven't even been made yet or give you surprising titles that may happen in theatres! That's why I must not show, even a glimpse, of this book: that would change history!"

I chuckled again, "OK, man who knows everything". I thought I was talking someone very strange who had the weirdest knowledge ever.

Then I was about to head back to the ceremony and leave this guy alone; but that would've been my biggest mistake.

The stranger took out an even stranger device. It was pretty colourful; it was pinkish purple with more pink than purple. It had red glowing lights that were making sounds to alert him.

"Ah! That's my cue," he said as he got off the bench.

With much intrigue, I walked back to him and asked, "Where did you say you were going?"

"Oh," he said, "I've been invited to an Admiral's ship. He said he wanted me for something".

"So that's why you're not formally attending here, but attending to something else", I said, as if I knew what this guy was talking about.

"Yes", he replied happily, "I thought I might kill time and sit here a bit".

"But why?" I asked him.

"Because its boring and simple", he replied, "anyway, its better than to wait in the waiting room".

"Let me guess:", I said, "its boring".

"No, its just that there's nothing interesting to look at. But yeah, I can take that".

I know, I just met this guy and chatted with him for about a minute. But there was something different about him, like he was looking for something; maybe I was looking for the same thing?

"Can I…can I come with you?" I asked him as if I was stupid.

He turned and shared a startled look, "Are you sure?" he said, surprised.

I thought about it carefully, and I gave it to chance. I nodded.

"The name's Floyd; what's yours?"

I glared at him, "Charlotte".

Floyd gave me the device with his hand and warned, "OK, where we will be going might cost you your life".

"I can manage," I responded.

"Good," he said, "because I don't want to be blamed if I told you so".

He pressed a button on the device, and we beamed away.

At that moment, I wondered if anyone would notice I might be away for a bit.

2) The Rose

It was like the coolest trip ever! We were just standing in the garden one moment, and then we travelled through some wormhole with flashing colours popping around us. It was beautiful but a bit hard on the eye. Then we arrived at some door in front of us.

Inside it was all high-tech stuff. The place had organ-iron metal around the room and a soft floor. It also seemed like the room was hexagonal. And the furniture looked convertible - very detailed and alien-like.

I wondered around, with many thoughts going through my mind. Like - what just happened, or this was amazing!

"Wh…where are we?" I asked in excitement.

"I just told you," Floyd said, confused as if he didn't say it as he clearly remembered, "we are inside the Admiral's ship, that he invited me to…".

Floyd recalled something as he walked over to a guest's package kit. He grabbed a very interesting amulet. And he handed it to me.

"Well," I said, "is this some kind of first date that I wasn't aware of?"

"This isn't just a teleporter but also an invitation to the Admiral's ship. If you don't wear one of these in there, you'll be a target enemy, and this ship will blast you into oblivion in minutes!"

I thought that would be a frightful experience and I didn't like to take my odds. I took the amulet and put it around my neck. "So, this is a spaceship?" I asked.

"Yes. You will believe me from now on?" he asked.

"What?" I asked.

"You thought I was making things up; what made you suddenly change your mind?"

I was kinda flashing through my mind as to how quickly I accepted this opportunity. "Well…I thought when you mentioned all the stuff you said, I just wanted to jump in and go with it".

Floyd turned to me with a curious face and, hoping that wasn't a bad thing, "You just jump in and go with it?"

"Yeah" I said, "look, sometimes you just have to go with something that is coming in your way, and the only way you can do it is to jump on it".

He was trying to figure out why I was willing to go with him. Sure, it was all happening so fast, but we were in space! I wanted to see my opportunities if this guy was telling the truth.

He later changed his expression as he shook it off. He realised it would have been a very interesting experience for me.

An alien of some kind came out of a door that opened sideways. He had a jaggy grey face with two horns on top, but I wasn't sure what the front four horns were on his face. He had deep red eyes with giggling teeth. He also had something going around his nose, but I was afraid to ask.

Oddly, he wore a basic dinner suit; at least some things don't entirely change from the human race.

"Admiral Keeill is waiting for you, Mr Librarian," he said, not in an aggressive voice, but one where you could say his side of the family undoubtedly meant business.

"You could call me Mr Surlen," Floyd added.

I whispered over to him to ask, "Is that surely your name?"

"Oh, no", he said, "I really have other names than that".

Then the ugly alien looked to me, "And who you might be Miss…?"

"…Surlen," I said stupidly; I wasn't focusing, all right?

"What?" Floyd said, as if I was stupid.

"No, I mean, I'm his sister," I said clearly.

"Uh," the alien spoke with his head nodding, "so, he'll be waiting for you".

We walked through a corridor with the same hexagonal shape; it was kind of different and weird, but it made a lot of sense if you saw any sci-fi movies or tv shows. It led to another door where we could see the Admiral's room through the door's small top window.

Another corridor on our left would lead us elsewhere, but we were sure he knew where we were going.

"So, who's this Admiral Keeill?" I asked Floyd.

"He is one of the greatest leaders of the Tale's Empire. He served over millions of soldiers in the biggest War that was fought on his home world".

I thought that summed everything up, "But why does he need you?"

Floyd gave me the "I don't know" expression that I understood very clearly. I'm mostly the master of well-known body language, as everyone said.

The alien butler guy opened the door with some code; he dialled it, and we walked in. We were at some dinner table, a more royal one than back at the wedding. It was a sleek black table, and the walls were dead red. We saw an open window at the back where we could see the galaxy. The Admiral was sitting in front of it and behind the dinner table.

I was thinking he must be the most show-off of all showoffs. This guy was trying to tick us off because he was the best.

He was different from the other alien. He was pinked-skinned, with things that weren't horns but something else; they were sticking up longer and were on the opposite side than the other guy. He also had a line marking on his forehead and gorgeous, light-yellow eyes.

He also wore Earth-like clothing. He was wearing clothes like an ordinary captain usually wore when he had a dinner party.

He smiled at us firmly. I wasn't sure what person we were about to meet, but he seemed somewhat friendly, I guessed.

"Welcome, my friend", he greeted Floyd in a not-so-much French accent mixed with brutish.

"Thank you for having us, Your Excellency", Floyd said as he bowed.

I bowed as well; what kind of person would I be if I hadn't done that to an alien Admiral whom I had just encountered on the day of my sister's wedding?

"It is also nice to meet you, you're…you're Excellency," I said shakily, trying to face it that I was seeing an alien, an actual alien! "I am Charlotte, Floyd's sister, as you will".

"And we'll discuss that later," Floyd said in an ordinary professional manner.

The Admiral welcomed us to take our seats as Floyd and I sat together.

"It is good to see you again, Floyd," the Admiral continued, "after helping me to look out for the Royal Kingdom's trophies".

"Nah, those kids don't know where to look like you do." Floyd complimented him, "Why did you bring me here now after all the adventures we've been on?"

Admiral Keeill leaned down and showed he was in desperate need. A hologram popped up revealing some object.

"Indeed, we've been through a lot, my friend." He agreed. "About three months ago, my wife's wedding gift, the Silver Rose, was lost in the vacuum of space; we have no clue where it ended up, but it seems to have arrived in this part of space".

We looked out into the open space; it looked like the Milky Way but orange with purple dust. We could almost see close planets nearby.

"The System of Trees?" Floyd noticed, as he had some knowledge of this.

The Admiral eyed him in agreement. "I sent a few of my personal Squires to find it, but they have failed. It is her royal treasure, and her royal treasure is my royal treasure."

My Royal Treasure? What sort of possession was this? Didn't anyone know about refunds or whatever?

"Floyd, if you find this, I'll pay you with whatever is in my bounty".

I would have taken that order right away! And I would have said, "Excuse me, sir, we just met. We'll take up the case, and I will take this case if Floyd doesn't have any other plans". But what happened instead was that Floyd just waved his arms and said, "All right, my friend", and they shook hands.

Wow, even tagging along, I wanted to sign up for the job. Hey, I wanted to be the one who was given that job!

3) Above the Trees

Me and Floyd walked over to the docking range where Admiral Keeill had given us a pod ship to use. The ship's interior was right behind another curvy shield door.

I wanted to look at Floyd, but for some reason, he seemed distracted. "What do you think you're doing?" I asked him.

"It's a new hobby I've been practising for quite some time now," he said while fiddling with his arm; or else I thought he might be having a stroke of some kind.

"Why did you take that offer very lightly?" I asked.

"Oh, it's no big deal," he said, "they will probably give me some army stuff or priceless jewels".

"That would be a big deal!" I said with shock.

"I don't really go for that kind of stuff", he tried to explain, "I don't want anything to do with it, I just normally go for the adventure, and that's that".

I thought that was a very pointless excuse. Anyone would've grabbed that offer if they wanted a glimmer of fame or power. But he just wanted to throw that out the window.

But when I thought of it, he made quite a lot of sense. It was all about the adventure, wasn't it? Maybe this guy knew what he was speaking about, but I still didn't guess what he was saying half of the time.

"On the other hand," he said, fiddling, "I normally do stuff like this rather than being rich".

He took out a magic trick card that he wanted to show me, "You see it?" then he moved his hands as the card disappeared, "now you don't!"

He magically "appeared" the same card again, "disappeared" it and repeated the same trick.

I knew he was going to repeat it forever.

"You can stop that," I said finally.

He stopped as a sackful of cards fell out of his sleeve. He was picking up his mess of cards on the shiny royal floor while I stepped inside the ship before we went.

Admiral Keeill could have thought of a nice ship that could go at light speed or see how this side of the galaxy was.

But what we got was a small and quiet ship that didn't have the best lighting. There wasn't much inside but a crowded space of furniture and cargo that someone had forgotten to put away. There was even a toilet on board, for crying out loud! But one I didn't know how to flush.

The piloting room, on the other hand, was even smaller. I could see this room from the main base, but Floyd was sitting on the one very comfortable chair, which I thought was selfish.

It seemed like he knew how to pilot this thing. He was stirring the ship as it was moving. Floyd said it was like basic controls, which was a straightforward tip. When you want to move left, you move left; you want to go up; you go up; if you want to move faster, you push forward on the joystick.

There were no buttons to press, no co-pilot or anything; you just move the joystick like in a jet, but more simpler than that (I think?).

It was very cool setting out where we were going. I looked around the open space of the galaxy again; the colourful dust kinda reminded me of tiny roots spreading outwards to reach towards the stars. Or so it was in this system.

"So, what kind of area of the galaxy are we going to?" I asked Floyd.

Floyd tried to lean his neck, but I had a feeling he couldn't move. "This range of space is, of course, connected with the life of nature itself".

He pointed to the root area I spotted before, "You see that?" he asked.

"Yes".

"That was the spine of a dying tree that lived four billion years ago. It is said it was forced to be cut down, as the tree grow larger than the planet. It weakened the planet as it was dying. They had to evacuate the population".

"That's sad", I added. I leaned over and asked, "Where are we going?"

Floyd looked at some star that wasn't too far, "Totano".

"And why are we going there?"

"It's the main planet in the system, and I've heard that's where we get our answer," he said with confidence.

We soon arrived at Totano. It was like a giant jungle, or we were like tiny ants. There were massive trees that were like Mount Everest size and others as big as its stepbrothers.

We couldn't see the ground clearly as smaller trees surrounded it. We sometimes saw houses and buildings on the giant trees. I thought I imagined that, but I knew I wasn't overthinking it.

They had platforms to help guide their way through their cities, but not harming the trees. At least somebody in the galaxy cared for mother nature.

There weren't a lot of cities nearby. Floyd said the one we were going to would be twenty trees away.

It wasn't quite the longest trip I was expecting. Just admiring the planet was enough for me. Floyd was enjoying himself flying, I could tell.

It was afternoon as the sun was getting low. We arrived at one of the cities that seemed so wooden. Everything was meant to be a pile of wood. Wood tunnels, wood wells, and the people themselves were wood too!

This was not creepy or weird, as you might expect. I kinda got used to the idea that we lived in a universe where the tree had its own space system and species.

As we landed, the pod ship docked with a row of other vessels that seemed like construct art, but they were ships.

I wondered about the city and admired the folks in the area. They looked fantastic, I say. I know I shouldn't stare as it was creepy, but these guys looked sick!

One guy had a moustache that was pulling down to his chin. Another was tall with long arms coming to its knee with claws. The children that ran past also had cool details.

"They…?" I asked.

"Foot-toes," Floyd said at a lamp post, "they, including this planet, were the leftovers of the giant tree".

"The one that died billions of years ago?" I asked. Floyd nodded.

I walked over to him, "So, has it been chopped? Did it also make life?"

"Oh yes," Floyd recalled, as if I asked the wrong question, "it created more life in more planets. That's why it's called the System of Trees. That tree made a system of itself with life among many stars".

Boy, whoever knew nature would connect like this on any other planet? I never thought it wanted to handshake the worlds and make life out of itself.

Then another question struck me, "Then that means those ships we saw out at the landing bay were from other planets in the System, right?"

"Correct!" Floyd replied as he spun around the lamp pole and fell down, "I say, you're getting the hang of this. Did you pay attention in your exams at school?"

"What?" I asked.

"You know? The whole galaxy and other things; you're like the perfect expert! You seem pretty OK with it?"

I blushed, "I watch too many tv shows".

Floyd gave me another severe stare, then just shrugged it off. I had no idea what that was about; I hoped I hadn't done anything wrong.

4) Unfamiliar Friends

The first Woodling we interrogated was one on a hilly street, where we could see the horizon and the landing bay. He was outside a clubhouse with a sign in a weird language that even Floyd could not make out the letters.

The weirdest thing was that the guy was creaking. I mean, he wasn't talking but creaking. "What's wrong with him?" I asked Floyd.

Floyd was listening very carefully to him as each creak that passed. The worst thing about it was that the wood guy made these horrifying expressions that scared me out.

"They don't really communicate in English" Floyd replied. "They speak in a tone that, like animals, others of their kind could only respond to".

"So, you're saying they're speaking in another language we can't understand?" I asked.

"Precisely," he said as he kept listening to the creaking wooden man.

We stood there for another few seconds; what I heard was creaking and a similar creaking as before. I had no clue if Floyd knew how to speak tree or what, but I would say, he was an excellent listener.

When the tree man stopped creaking, he turned around and left us. Floyd's eye turned towards me, "He said he knows a guy who knows the whereabouts of the Rose".

"Yes!" I said gladly. I don't know how he managed it, but I was relieved.

"But he said it's on another planet".

"Oh", I said, not sure what to think.

The only problem that lay on my mind was home; what if I spent too long away from home? But again, we were just talking to wood people, so how could I miss that?

Before we kept going, we heard someone panic. We already knew trees didn't scream, and mostly everyone here was a tree.

What was coming our way through a tunnel was a figure in a hoody. I didn't think he was human, either, looking at it. He looked robotic with metal. The face was covered by a hood, the same as the thing he was carrying.

"I TOLD YOU NOT TO BE SEEN!" the bag said in a robotic voice.

When I turned to Floyd, his face was frightened, and I had some weird feeling that he knew what all this was about. The figure took off its hood and showed an orb-looking face with another of the same orb in his hand.

He walked to us and stopped. "WHERE HAVE YOU BEEN!!!" the orb said directly to Floyd.

"Do you know them?" I asked.

Floyd's expression didn't change much, "Ah, not quite, really".

"WHEN YOU SAID YOU WANTED TO GO OUT FOR A VISIT, I DIDN'T GET THE MEMO YOU WOULD NEVER RETURN TO THE LIBRARY!"

"I was going to go back", Floyd blushed, "things just got in the way of things".

"YEAH, WHEN I WAS SHOT AT!" the orb angered, "YOU COULD HAVE TOLD ME THAT!"

"Yes…" Floyd said slowly, "but I gave YO-NO the news".

"YEAH, HE HAS BEEN A GREAT HELP".

"Has he?"

"OF COURSE NOT! HE HAS BEEN TAKING ME IN THE WRONG DIRECTION TO FIND YOU!"

Floyd squished his face like he was about to face trouble big time.

"THIS GUY HAS LITTLE FUNCTION, SO IT WAS DIFFICULT TO GUIDE HIM THROUGH ALL THIS TROUBLE!"

"DISANATSION-7809.139-EVERYTHING IS SO UNDERCONRTOL-BY MY BEST PAL, LO-NO," said the robot.

"SEE?" LO-NO tried to explain the issue, "EVEN HE DOESN'T KNOW WHERE HIS AT!"

"SOUP".

"WHAT?"

"SOUP HAS BEEN DETECTED; WE MUST GET SOME SUPPLIES".

YO-NO took off with LO-NO while Floyd and I just watched them go off.

"NO! THAT WAS IN YOUR CODE?" LO-NO said, trying to get YO-NO back into shape, "GO BACK! WE MUST GET THE LIBRARIAN! GO BACK I ORDER YOU!"

Then as they walked down the hill, there were no longer any interferences from the robots.

Man, I wondered how Floyd got into their skins?

We later headed to the guy who knew where the Silver Rose was. We were at the centre of the city's tree, and we saw a row of Woodlings connected to the tree. It was pretty terrifying, with their facial expressions frozen. One was happy about how his fate turned out; one was quite frightened of the horrors he was facing as he realised this was not his idea.

I mean, Man! this place was wonderful and all, but why do the Woodlings have to creep me out so much?!

"Man," I said in horror, "do we know which one we're talking to?"

"What I have heard is that this is the one", Floyd replied, as we looked at the one in front of us. His expression was pale, like a guy we saw sitting in a back lane.

"Are you sure?" I said, not trying to unrespect the dead. Or, rather, wondering if they were dead.

The creaking started again. He didn't change his facial expression as he creaked along, and I knew where this was going all over again. I kinda wanted to move things forward.

"So, what was that story with the robots?" I asked Floyd next to me.

Floyd shared an unsure look with a bit of guilt. I could tell whatever he did, it must've been really bad.

"There was a thing; we dealt with the thing, but a teacher shot him as she was working with lizard pirates who wanted to tear the fabric of space".

"Ah," I said, a bit unsure, "and you work at a Library?"

"No, I guard a Library, as there isn't anyone else to do the job".

"No one?"

"Its complicated", he said as I took his word on it.

"And you left those robot things to do the job for you?"

"Yeah, for the moment".

"It must be pretty serious".

"Yeah…" he said carefully, "I'll go back. One day".

Then after Floyd focused on the creaking, he turned away and took off. "I know where we are going".

We were on our way towards the landing bay, somewhere in a street with buildings on each side where we were walking. On one the side of the street, there was some deal with a bunch of woodlings surrounding something or someone.

Me and Floyd tried to look at what was going on in that crowd, and we saw those same robots, LO-NO and YO-NO, and I could tell they were in trouble, BIG TIME.

"I ORDER YOU! WE MUST FIND FLOYD!" LO-NO tried to talk sense into his robot partner, with whom he had no formal relationship other than being in his arms.

"CHEESE, THE FORMAL FABRIC OF LIFE. CHEESE MAKES EVERYTHING. CHEESE IS EVERYTHING," the broken robot replied.

"NO IT ISN'T!!!!!"

We thought something bad was going down.

Floyd suggested, "Time to go," and we did.

5) The Problem of Falling

Floyd never quite told me about where we were going after we left Totano. He said he was going to tell me when we got back to the ship, but he never brought it up.

With every minute I got to know him, something new popped out of nowhere. Which helped me to learn more about him. Maybe these facts weren't true, but who's really to judge, huh? Who wanted to judge?!

We were speeding at light speed through the colourful stars, and we saw a brand-new light in the cosmos. Sharp pink flares were flying across through glowing stars, and it was like sliding into space. The luminous stars were chasing after the runaway flare as I just watched while Floyd set us on our next course.

It was hard to tell where we were. It took us several hours to reach our destination. Maybe for one, because our ship was slow.

But it was in a different part of space. Floyd said this was on the edge of the System at the far corner of the Tree System. I wondered if anyone was put on these planets at the back - if they did something wrong.

Mean.

The planet was dark when we reached it. Like something pretty bad had happened to it. But when we came to land, the planet lightened up, and it looked strange when we landed. It had the same typical sky as Earth, but nothing else seemed to be like that. What we were soon about to stand foot on…was gravel?

Floyd took one step on the ground of gravel. It was so strange, it felt like stepping on ground full of stuffed up teddy bears.

The landscape was straight, no hills, nothing.

Sometimes I could barely tell what I was stepping on.

"We're on gravel?" I asked Floyd.

Floyd was full of intrigue and might have never been on a planet like this before.

OK. OK, OK, OK. In this part of the story, you might say my day couldn't get any more weird, and you're not wrong; but things just get more hectic from here!

Today I had met Woodlings, aliens with horns, robots, creatures that can plug into the tree like a power-point, and I was standing on gravel and it felt weird. But I was interested in my surroundings, and nothing was going to stop me there.

"Yeah, but with surprises that I'm trying to figure out," Floyd called out, still moving around strangely like I was.

It wasn't like normal gravity; something was trying to pull me into the ground.

"So, this is it, yeah?" I asked as we walked through the fields.

"Mostly", he responded.

I looked around as stars above tried to blind me, "So…planet Gravel?"

"Ah, I wouldn't quite say that," he said, trying to turn around, "Before we landed, I found a source".

"What source?"

"A source. A source that is inside the planet," he said with precision. "There's something more to this planet than what we're seeing".

The only thing that came into my head was, "Oh, how do we do that?"

When I spoke that, I sank into the ground. I mean, right into the gravel. And I thought I was having problems with where I would step next!

I screamed as Floyd turned to where I fell. "Charlotte!" he cried, "Where are you?"

"I'm stuck," I said inside the gravel. I couldn't tell how to take the whole experience; I just wanted to get out as I fiddled.

"Then…can you get unstuck, please?" he asked politely.

I didn't respond because then I really sank underneath the surface of the planet.

It was scary, weird, and a bit painless. I dropped inside some soft, rocky hills below. Well, at least I thought they were hills, anyway.

I woke up and noticed that I fell six thousand feet, which should have killed me, or the gravel at least. Why didn't the sinking gravel kill me?

But I had other problems on my mind. Where was I? Where was Floyd? My ticket back home?

When I was thinking with a million things in my head, I looked at my amulet: it was dead like a phone. That was a relief, I thought.

The place looked distended; and I mean, nobody would ever want to come here and chill. The hills looked rough; they had piles of the gravel that might have fallen down here. Where I was sitting was a bit weirder. It was like an ordinary stone hill, but when I took a closer look at it, it had purple wood skin under it, like it was part of another material.

When I thought this couldn't get any worse, there came a roar, and it shook the ground, hills, me and everything miles and miles away. Nobody could not notice that.

I hid behind a stone/wood wall that was near to me. It was torn apart by something. Mostly like everything else here.

When I turned my head in a frightened mood, what I saw was a creature. A creature that was difficult to look at. Its body had spirals going around like rings. It had a glowing floating red eye where the head should be; its vision had a scanning red light as it watched over the place.

Its height was as huge as an office building, with a fearsome feel that you knew you could only have two options: A) don't even think to approach it and stay where you are, or B) get the hell out of there!

I was frightened in my bones, and I knew I couldn't face it. What I also saw near it were giant statues of ancient creatures. One that looked like a lizard, and others I couldn't explain what species they were (but I bet Floyd could if he was here).

You may want to know what I did next? Nothing special till this guy shows up.

He was strolling over the other side on another hill. He had those skull animal heads with horns, with a chain mail that covered his neck. At least he was wearing a shirt, but he didn't have sleeves, which I thought was weird.

"Hey, you!" he said to the massive and scary-looking monster, "Yeah? Want a piece of me?"

The creature growled at him as the guy quickly ran down the hill. Yeah, I thought angrily, you better run.

Then other men and creatures came and charged at the creature. They had battle armour and weapons as they charged. One dude was blue with four arms and had a junk of stuff on him.

As they all headed up the hill, the light of the creature's eye darkened its light; as for the rescue party, they stopped as they held still and kneeled in pain from the light. And the worst part was, they turned to dust as they dropped like sand.

I gasped, and the next thing was the same dude I mentioned before, the skull-headed dude, came over to me and covered my mouth to shush me.

"Don't worry," he said in a French accent, "I know the way".

He held out his hand from my mouth; I slapped him and then hit him, "What. Were. You. Thinking!" I said to him, angry.

"But I still do know the way," he said as he took my hand and rushed down the hill.

What we saw nearby on a shorter hill was a box-shaped elevator. "Is that it?" I asked the guy.

He nodded, "Yep! We have to go!"

As we kept running down, the monster came over to where we were and was aware of us. Its light was coming toward us. We turned our heads in horror.

"Oh no", skull head said hopelessly, "it's the nectar!"

"What?" I said, but he just shut up, and we kept moving.

I had no clue who this guy was, but he surely didn't have a thing with greetings. He hadn't shaved his face for some time as bits of hair from his beard was still hanging, and he had a dark beard on the tip of his chin, Totally unattractive. He had light blue eyes and a very rich French accent.

We marched forward to the elevator as the light reached onto us. The guy was pushing the iron door to open it; I turned back to the creature's bright light, wanting this guy to move fast.

He pushed open the door and got me inside. I got inside of the elevator as the light started to harm him. he was struggling and I knew I couldn't leave him here. I wouldn't feel the same if I let someone die on my watch.

I pulled him in and pressed a button as the door closed. But when I thought that would be the end, the elevator dropped fast. I thought I was done falling; I am afraid I was wrong.

6) The Woolly and Smashing Rescue

Now, where were we? Oh! We dropped once again. But we luckily arrived at a stop. What I mean by that was we were still alive; well, mostly. I say it was more of a heavy landing from which we had a few bruises but nothing more harmful than that.

The elevator was busted when we dropped and dust splattered our clothes. I took the guy who saved me out and pulled him over to a wall.

As I wasn't sure how far we dropped this time; I bet we fell much further than last time. I couldn't tell how deep we were.

I could hear a typical street ahead. We were sitting in a modern-day corridor where a regular elevator should be.

Besides the dusted face he had from the fall, his eye was dripping with sweat, and he was tired from the excursion.

I had my theory that whatever the beam of light was, it must've not only caused harm to a person but drained them, like if you were going for a run in very extreme weather.

He put on a smile for me while I was checking on him. "Don't you worry", I tried to be confident, "I'll check if anything's wrong".

"Hey", he said, as his voice was dying down, "It's OK. It's just a bruise".

I wasn't sure if he was being cattish or telling the truth. I had to make my mind up whether he was going to die or not.

"You sure?" I pulled my head closer.

"Yes", he said. He sighed as he put his head on the wall and closed his eyes.

I didn't know what to do. I left him at peace, I guess. I walked out towards the mysterious neighbourhood I was about to wander into.

To be honest, I still had no idea where to go now. The street was very fictional, with unusual faces popping in and out.

It was a very Victorian town as the folks wore like the worst version of clothes of that era. They wore Victorian with strange patches and other details on them. They had other clothing that didn't match; well, nothing matched on them.

The street came to curl in a wonky way; I wasn't sure if I was in the same place as I had been.

There were some folks that crawled through the walls to get into places that I thought were freaky. I even saw ones that were jumping onto the buildings. But the strange thing about that was these folks were mostly alien-like. There weren't any humans I saw here, but they weren't quite alien either.

The other weird thing I also noticed was at one edge, the end of the street, there was nothing there but a massive stone wall with a tunnel and a river that went somewhere.

But there was the fact I had to face. I was lost. I was way past Floyd right now, and I just got saved by a complete stranger - I didn't even know his name.

"There's no sky", said Floyd, who was on the other side of the street from me.

I walked over to him in relief, "Floyd!" I called, but he was distracted.

"Oh, hi!" he said as he turned to look at me, "Don't you notice it seems to be dark? Very dark?"

I wasn't aware it was dark, but he wasn't kidding; the street was nothing but a dark, creepy, weird Victorian city, except for the lamps.

"Yeah, you're right", I agree with him as a question came to me, "How did you get here?"

"Oh! I've come the other way".

I pause, "What other way?"

"Well, let's say I had help" he seemed like he was lying.

"I almost died!"

"OK, I had a little help. I just ended up going the same way you did".

I didn't have the words to say to him. I frowned at him and later shook that off. We were both in big situations, and I shouldn't blame him. But I was happy we were back together, safe and sound.

While I was glad to find him again, I spotted two folks in goggles. One had a hoody and a staff-like mask to cover his face. The other one didn't. He snarled at us, and they took off.

I looked back at Floyd and asked him, "Where do you think we should go?"

We strolled over the street, and we didn't know where we might go next. We arrived at an alleyway that told us we may be killed on the spot.

"Who was this guy who suddenly saved your life?" I asked him. Floyd turned back to me with curiosity. "Oh, come on! You had an easy pick to get here! Who saved you?"

"Someone named Mr Nail".

"Oh".

"But goes by the name Fully Fartsome Nail".

"Ah," I said, "so where's your stormy Knight now?"

Floyd showed me a door right on the other side in front of us. We could also see a large window inside, which was very easy to see.

When we stepped inside, we were in a post office with shelves of mail inside. It was several feet tall with a few ladders scattered over the place.

"Incredible!" I called out. Then in front of me was an alien that looked like a lion. His face was human-like, but his beard was golden and big.

He was wearing a purple sweater and a dressing robe, which reminded me a bit of Floyd. He had pants, too but wasn't bothered with any slip-on shoes.

"You must be Mr Nail?" I said, preferring to take that name than his first two.

He glared at Floyd, "I presume you wish to tell me who this is?"

Floyd went over to his ear as Mr Nail understood everything, "Ah, so, you were both separated".

"You didn't tell him about me?!" I shouted at Floyd.

"I…I didn't mean to," Floyd tried to confess.

"I did save him, but I couldn't reach you, young lady," Mr Nails said in a very rich tone.

Floyd and I looked at him as we had a few more questions to ask him.

"Where are we, exactly?" I asked, "and who are those people out there? They aren't people, are they?"

The golden beard man reached over to his table, pouring wine into his glass.

"To your first question: this is the Bark. It is a world where we discovered many unknown places we never knew we could reach, some we may never discover yet".

"To your second question," he turned to us, "we are Bonlers".

"A what?" I asked.

Floyd whispered in my ear, "They are aliens that cross with other aliens".

"That's a bit hard, isn't it?" I commented to Floyd when I remembered what they were like. They were like test experiments gone wrong; how could this ever happen?

"Our lives aren't anything than easy" Mr Nail handed me and Floyd a glass of whatever was in it. Floyd tried to drink it, but it wasn't his suit, so he spat it back in.

"Folks roam through these streets, trying to learn who they are. Some are savage, some are misfits trying to make a life on their own, and some just do whatever they like".

Seemed confusing, I thought. Walking through a street with strange creatures who don't even know where they came from and trying to kill you was not a pleasant thought.

"What do they want?" I spoke.

Mr Nails gave another unpleasant look, "nothing really. Only for them to understand who they are".

"and how's that going?" Floyd asked.

"Pretty terrible, if you ask me", Mr Nails thought, "We really don't have a government. Which makes the issue ten more times tougher. There have been some rogues through the Bark who have been keeping them in check".

"Rogues?", I asked which kinda reminded me about the guy who saved me and his other pals, "I think I've encountered them on the way here".

"Really?", Floyd asked as he seemed interested.

"Yeah, some guy came and saved me. But are there more of them?"

"Of course", Mr Nails said, "there's bunch of them wondering through the Bark as we speak. They have their own desires and duties. They are normally the ones who have a clear understanding of what they are".

"Through the Bark?", Floyd asked, "Tell us more about that?"

A banging came from a room near us.

"Pardon me," Mr Nail said as he walked in and closed the door. We could hear it seal shut.

I tried not to disturb him, but I could hear him talking to somebody. Gosh, what he was saying was true? I couldn't tell if I trusted him; even though the look of him seemed like a nice guy, I had a bad gut feeling inside me.

I turned to Floyd, "We should go".

"Why?" he asked me, surprised.

"I don't trust him".

"With a welcome greeting, you think he wanted ..." Floyd froze as he thought ahead, "Ooooh...".

"There's something not right about all of this," I told him.

"The weather?" Floyd asked.

"No," I couldn't pick out what, but something really rang to me, making me want to get out now, "we should get out of here".

We stepped out of the house and were stopped by a bunch of unpleasant folk who popped up alongside us like goggle brothers. They hissed around us, and it looked like they were going to eat us.

"You're not going to eat us, are you?" I asked them, even though I wasn't sure if they were alien or animal. But I forgot it didn't matter; they were something completely different.

Floyd shook nervously, "I…I'll warn you!" he said with no weapon or plan.

They laughed. We weren't sure we could get away from them that easily.

"Maybe we go back inside," I said.

"But you said we should go out?" Floyd replied, confused. "What do you want to do? Get killed or later get killed?"

Then, Mr Nail came out to the street and said, "What is the meaning of this?!"

He moved right in front of us, and these strangers moved back.

"Get out of here!" he told them off.

But one of them sneakily jumped on Mr Nail and he fell to the floor. Mr Nail tried to move, but he struggled to get the man off him. He glared at us to do one thing, "Go! Save yourselves!"

"But how?!" Floyd replied hopelessly, "we're dead like the situation you're in!"

Then a random thing happened. The walls behind him in his house smashed and collapsed on the aliens. Brick by brick, they couldn't escape.

What smashed the wall was a mammoth, an actual mammoth! And two dudes were riding it. The one at the front had a goat head who didn't look much, and another one had an owl head, but he was masculine with no shirt.

I could not tell what me and Floyd were seeing. But to summarise, we were saved by a mammoth, a goat, and an owl with abs.

"Get on!" said the owl, who somehow spoke English. We got onto the mammoth like we were told.

Then one of the aliens tried to get on, "Get off the mammoth!" Floyd called out as he pushed him off.

The mammoth headed forward, got out of the alleyway, and made way through the street.

We were clashing through the street with folks in the way. What we could do was tell everyone to get out of the way. Thankfully they listened as they took notice of our wild fury diversion.

As the mammoth stomped over through the street, it hit light poles and walls of buildings. Soon crates and pie shops,

Not the Pie shops! I thought; my grandpa worked at a Pie shop.

We made our way as we did, but we couldn't stop the dang mammoth. But everyone was just in the way. It was out of control! It was soft but very strong.

While we were figuring out how to stop it, we noticed a river on the other side which our mammoth was heading towards.

"Pull it!", said the owl guy.

"What?!", I replied.

"Pull all together!", Floyd said, as he seemed to get the idea. I followed his lead as I had no idea what I was doing.

We pulled the mammoth all together, including the goat who looked terrified about the whole experience.

With a big hassle, we held back. The mammoth stopped its crashing just as a small lamp pole sparked, and we were just a few feet from the river.

As we were catching our breaths, we realised we were lucky that our first full mammoth ride came right when we needed it.

7) The Door

We turned towards a quiet street passing by a bridge over the river. There were some folk around, but they didn't care what we were doing on an ancient creature from a billion years ago that somehow popped over here.

We reached the other end of the city; the buildings were aimed close towards the giant brick wall that circled around the entire city like a dome. But where we were felt curious; there was something odd about this part of the city. I couldn't tell what made me feel or even think of that, but something was afoot, as great authors say.

I was the last one to get off the mammoth as I wasn't sure how to get off it. Floyd was the only one who helped me; as for the weird animal heads, they just took off inside one of the buildings without care.

Floyd held out his arms as I dropped on him. "Thanks," I said, "what was all that about?"

"Beats me," he said, having no clue.

I looked at the house; it was small with expansive windows on each side. It was also a tight place to stay, and next to it was a small garage for the mammoth as it entered.

"Do you think they really meant to save us or was it just another thing?"

"Could be another thing", Floyd responded honestly, "but I think Mr Nail wanted them to save us".

I felt pretty bad for Mr Nail. As much as his first names were tough, he did save our lives, and I shouldn't be suspicious of him as if he was going to kill us in the process.

I asked Floyd, "Who are those guys, anyway?"

"Don't know", he replied, "I say if they were chilling at Mr Nail's place, it would mean we should trust them".

"Should we?" I asked that same question before. "I mean. I believed Mr Nail at the time he saved us, but these are bozos who ride a mammoth like idiots. Should we go with them?"

Floyd looked at the house we were going to go into, then looked at me. "As Mr Nails knew his way, I would say they do too," as he walked over to the door where they went.

I wanted to stay put, but I knew I would die out here. So, I followed him in.

We arrived at a cosy lounge; it had furniture over a long soft woolly carpet that was neat with patterns.

There was a construct of some creatures on the ceiling. It seemed like other creatures than those I was aware of. For a moment, I thought there was a portrait of the owl and the goat fighting a ten-headed snake.

"Is this all yours?" I asked them. The owl was chilling on the couch in relaxation; the goat just sat down on the carpet with his legs crossed.

"Nah," said the goat.

I looked surprised, "So no?" I asked.

"Nah".

"He meant this isn't ours," replied the owl, "we were welcomed here by the great Gatekeeper".

"The Gatekeeper?" I tried to ask Floyd, but he was looking further into the house.

I turned back to my strange new friends, "Anyway, you live here?"

"Auhhhhh", called the goat.

The owl understood him and looked back at me. "He said we were wonderers like everyone else here. But we had a purpose. To explore and find duties in these unknown tunnels".

"Tunnels?" I asked as if I should know what they were.

"There are many paths inside the Bark; I believe you should have come by few?"

I came to think of it, "Actually, I have".

"These tunnels are all over the place", the owl explained, "it can take you about anywhere in the Bark".

"Anywhere?" I asked as I wondered how and where I could find one.

The owl closed his eyes and chuckled, "I'm sorry about my friend. He cannot speak your language; he is in a complex state of his forming".

The goat lay on the floor and sighed and thought of the carpet as the grass of his imagination. He knew it wasn't, but he wished it was.

He moaned at his Owl friend, "No, I put some in the refrigerator. No, he is in there".

"The Gatekeeper?" I asked.

The owl nodded, "He doesn't prefer other names. The Gatekeeper knows the way of the Bark. He and Mr Nail were the only ones who knew the place quite well enough, inside and out".

"Can we go through inside?" I tried to say.

The goat moaned again loudly.

"I would say that; it wouldn't be for me to say", the owl replied dimly, as it wasn't an option.

I wanted to wish these guys well as I got up, "What do they call you two?"

The owl stared for a couple of seconds, just before the goat went to sleep. "They call me Marshall, and this is my partner Loster. We are Guardians of the Spirits".

"Oh," I said.

"Nah, we made that up".

"Oh", I bowed and left them be.

I went to look for Floyd. I walked past a tight small hallway with a wooden floor. I soon saw a door on my left with an extensive wide see-through window where I could see someone inside the room.

He was sitting at a desk. Listening to some jazz on the radio. He was about sixty at least, with a long white beard coming down, small stuffy hair that had a little life yet, and wearing sunglasses.

He was reading papers that were all over the place. I mean, the place looked like a mess. The room he was in was half his study, with a sink and a refrigerator.

I thought, in realisation in a quiet and small gasp, "The Gatekeeper".

"The what?" asked Floyd coming through the other side of the hall.

I jumped in surprise; I hid what I said and asked, "What are you doing?"

"Just exploring the area," he said in amazement, "It's amazing! I think LO-NO would stop harassing me if I could work here".

I wasn't sure what Floyd was saying. What was his deal with that robot and that Library? "Why did you leave the Library?" I asked him.

"Well, it's a long story", Floyd said as he tried to move on from another subject.

"Okay", I said again, "why did you leave the Library?"

His facial expression expressed his mood, "I wanted to discover and explore. But LO-NO keeps telling me I've got responsibility for the Library".

"Then why didn't you go back?", again, his expression wasn't telling me much.

"I plan to", he said, quite unsure, "but he wouldn't understand. The cosmos is so wide and massive, and it just wanted to leave you guessing what's there. What's there to experience, an escape, but he doesn't have any understanding about imagination".

"Because he was programmed without any fun?" I asked.

"No, he has plenty of that", Floyd explained. "He has been programmed to annoy me".

Floyd looked at me till our eyes matched.

"Isn't it wonderful?" he said.

I actually agreed with him. All this exploring and discovering was truly wonderful. The planets, the aliens, all the frightful things and beauty across the galaxy.

I do see why someone like Floyd wanted to escape from a pasty robot to see something quite amazing in anyone's lifetime; I can agree with that.

"Yeah, you're right", I said as I made a small chuckle, "how can you ever think this is totally normal?"

"I don't", he replied, "I still can't get my head around the goat, though".

"and the mammoth", I said with a laugh, "how could it get all the way out here?"

"No, that I can imagine".

"Then, what else don't we know about this planet?", I asked Floyd as it was worth bringing up, "we still haven't found the Rose".

"I'm working on that", Floyd mentioned, as it sounded like he had been doing a bit of brainstorming.

"Since we arrived, the signal on our amulets went stone dead. But I can tell its far away where we need to be".

"Meaning?…".

"Meaning its not in this town".

"Great", I sighed.

"But its still in the Bark".

"Then where is it?", I asked, as I didn't think I could afford to be annihilated or get killed on the street again, "How big is this world?!"

"Don't know", Floyd said uncertain, "but if we dig deep enough, more deep than anything we can dig from…".

Then, I noticed the door behind Floyd at the end of the hall. Floyd followed my gaze as we stared at it and thought of the same exact thing.

"Are you sure?" Floyd stared at me.

I walked over to the door; it looked so old with its dark brown oak; it had a golden label on the top with some scrambled letters.

I held on to the golden doorknob and turned. When I turned the knob, the only result I got was a lock. I tried to pull again.

I turned back to Floyd, "It's not happening".

Floyd sighed, "Maybe there's another way for getting in".

We didn't really know what the time was. But if I guessed, it was close to being eleven. The street was darker, and I could barely see any light.

We were back in the lounge room with goat head and owl muscle. I saw a door open from the garage into the lounge room where the mammoth was sleeping.

I was still thinking about that door in the hallway. I couldn't shake it out of my mind. It was lying out there, staring at me. Like a golden light showing me something.

Floyd was reading news articles from the room and was making paper things. Maybe some kind of new magic trick, I guess.

"Do you know what's through that door in the hall?" I asked the owl.

He gave me a startled stare. His best pal was still sleeping with a big snore.

"You should really keep it down," he told me quietly, "nobody must know what's through there".

Floyd was looking at us suspiciously.

"Please", I said to Marshall.

"Even if I knew, nobody really knows what's in there other than the Gatekeeper himself".

"Then who's the Gatekeeper?"

The owl went silent as he had no plan to give out his full identity.

"The Gatekeeper is a secret man", he said.

"I can see that."

I told Marshall I remembered seeing the man in the study room earlier.

The owl gave me a scared and serious glare which was warning me. "You must know, the Bark is no place for anyone to wonder about in. There are dangers, dangers beyond your wild thoughts that would eat you alive. My only advice for you is, stay away from it, or at least from him".

I guessed I could wander inside his private study and ask him for permission, but I knew that would cause a lot of trouble for us.

I had to see it again. The lights were off, and everybody was asleep. And me and Floyd headed through the hall.

I was holding an old-fashioned candle in the dark.

"Is this so necessary?" Floyd asked.

"Yes!" I whispered to him. We wondered to the hallway, and we saw the door again. But this time, it was half open. We could see a bright light through it. We also noticed the Gatekeeper's room's light was out.

I couldn't tell if the guy went to bed or what, but me and Floyd thought to keep our low profile.

I turned to Floyd as he narrowed an eyebrow at me. He crept slowly to the door, and I stopped when we were close to it. Floyd walked over to it and pushed the door to slide it open.

I walked over to see what he was looking at. He dropped his jaw as I dropped mine.

What we saw was quite…(ahem)…a lot. We were on a floor of massive stairs that went on forever. It had the same wooden floor and the same materials as the rest of the house, but it just didn't stop. It was the hugest thing ever and the most dangerous.

We looked up and down as it went much further into the depths. I gulped and spoke, "Wow," in a lower voice.

I was totally astonished; if you have ever been to the strangest place in your entire life, try checking this out.

"What are you doing?!" said a voice behind us. As we turned, we were faced by a surprised and angry old man who glared at us with golden eyes through his sunglasses.

8) Guide Tour of The Bark

The lights were turned on in the lounge as Marshall and Loster woke up from their sleep. Floyd and I were confronted by an old man with sunglasses. Trying to be cool but trying without the angry look.

We made our way into the room while the Gatekeeper tried to be as terminating as ever.

"Why were you going through the stairs?" he asked us angrily.

"We, uh," I shyly said, as I couldn't get the words out. How could you, when you have encountered things you couldn't explain, while being put on trial by a man that glowed yellow in his eyes?

"This is a serious matter," he snapped as he went right to our faces with his severe glare, "Very. Serious. Matter".

He turned his back on us rudely, which I thought was fair enough.

"What are they?" he said to his pets, "Thieves? Robbers? Trespassers? Traitors?"

"They're friends of Mr Nail!" Marshall spoke nervously.

The Old man waved his hand to him, "I don't want to hear it" he refused the owl and looked back at us, "Why are you here?"

We weren't sure how to speak. We thought we were about to have a gun shot through us soon enough.

Before continuing his rampaging lectures, which I didn't want to hear, he studied us with his eyes squinted.

"I haven't seen your kind before?" he asked, as he tested us. "You're not Bonler. You are outsiders?"

Floyd wasn't sure what to do; I was the first to nod my head. The old man put his sunglasses back on and tried to be cool.

"I am sorry," he said, as me and Floyd sighed with relief. He soon went over to Marshall. "Why did you bring guests? You know I don't allow guests! Or like them".

"It was tight timing, sir", Floyd explained, walking up to him. "We really have a tight schedule and all that. We have come for the Silver Rose".

When Floyd brought it up, I had completely forgotten about the Rose. We were too busy going all over the place, and the only reason we were here was to find this particular object.

The Old man gasped in shock. I thought he was going to collapse. "The Silver Rose?" he said, covering his face. "The Rose!"

"Wait, you don't mean 'THE ROSE'?" said Marshall, standing up. Even the goat went over the top hearing the secret.

"Ah, yeah?" I said.

"Boy", Marshall replied, down struck.

"Then you're out of luck," The Gatekeeper said grimly, "you had better be off on your way than dying in there".

"Dying in what?" Floyd asked.

"The Rose is trapped in the place of all forgetting; nothing goes in or out".

What he said didn't sound so terribly bad to me.

"But it's what's on the way", Marshall warned, horrified. "You need to survive the most terrifying creatures alive. It is at the centre of the Spin-Can Tunnels".

Floyd turned away as he thought he was going to throw up.

"Spin-Can? What's a Spin-Can?" I asked them.

"A Spin-Can would be the last thing you would ever want to see", Floyd told me. And where was he when I almost died by that thing from above?

"How could a Spin-Can be that terrifying?" I asked, fearing the worst.

"Think about a spider".

"Yeah?"

"But a spider that had a step-father you could barely look at".

So what? I was about to meet the spider's worst father. It still wouldn't change my mind. I would take anything that could hit me!

"I don't care," I said, "we're going down there, and that's that".

Floyd knew he wouldn't bail out, even because of a scary monster that would wait for him and kill him.

It was the next morning when we went down the deep stairs into the abyss. I mean, gee, it was very steep as we walked. There were a bunch of doors on every single floor when we walked down. It had the same scattered letters, and I still couldn't tell what they meant.

It wasn't dark; everything was very bright and very clear. These could be doorways to other parts inside the Bark we could travel to.

Me and Floyd were led by the Gatekeeper, and Loster, who wanted to come along. The Gatekeeper had a staff with a glowing lamp on the top; it helped us when we travelled further through the stairs.

It took us hours to walk down to where we were meant to go. We stopped at one of the floors the Gatekeeper showed us.

"Behold!" he spoke with all glory, but it sounded like bad acting to me.

He pushed open the door, and we walked in. We walked through a small tunnel, and on the other side, we were at a docking ring in the dark. The dock was all stone craft made with a single lantern on a pole.

The ground we were walking on was brushed grass which seemed nature-like.

I wasn't sure where we were, but I noticed something about the river that seemed familiar.

"Is that the same river as before?" I asked.

"It is," said the Gatekeeper, "it leads all across the Bark as a link between ruins".

"What?" Floyd asked as if he didn't hear.

"Ruins".

"Ruins?"

"Yes".

"You said Ruins?"

"Yes!" the Gatekeeper repeated, "is that a problem?"

"Nah," Floyd commented.

"Good", the Gatekeeper replied, "because I would clobber you with my staff".

I laughed, and then I saw a small boat. It was a small rowboat, and someone was on it. When I saw who was on it as he held up his head. At that moment, I thought, "You!!!"

It was that guy who saved me. The one who wore a skull on his head, no sleeves, and I thought he was dead. No, he was alive this whole time and smiling at me.

"Oh, it's you!" he said with his French accent.

"This is Gravely," the Old Man said.

"I prefer Grad".

"Well, you are Gravely", the Gatekeeper continued, "He will take you into the Tunnels, but I warn you, you'll be back in bones".

The old guy walked back to the door and closed it behind him in farewell.

"Well, thank you!" I said scantily.

Floyd was still frightened; he knew he didn't want to go with it. He wanted to report back to Admiral Keeill and say the mission was a failure. But I was dragged too deep into this to go home.

Floyd stared at his amulet he was still wearing while I grabbed his hand, "What are you doing?"

"Haven't you just heard?!" Floyd panicked, "These things will haunt you in nightmares! Tear you into shreds and bones! But mostly bones!"

"But you want to get that Silver Rose, right?" I tried to talk Floyd into it.

"Yeah, before I knew Spin-Cans were involved" Floyd wanted to go with it, but he was full of terror. "Charlotte, you have no idea what we'll be walking into".

"Okay, okay", I said, thinking, "I'll look out for you. We'll be out sooner than we could expect".

Floyd gave me a small smile, "Thanks...".

I turned back to the fool that made a fool out of me. I was angry at him like either me or him was an idiot. He waved his hand to me with that same silly smile.

"Hi ya" he said happily.

He rowed us across the river in darkness. The river was still dark blue, like back at the city, and it was swishing in no direction. It took us on an easy road to where we were going.

Me and Floyd were sitting together, and Loster was on the other side of us. Grad was behind us, rowing with his row. He knew his stuff, and I was looking at him, trying to believe he was alive.

Floyd looked back at him and me repeatedly as he tried to understand our situation, "Do you know him?" he asked me.

I didn't want to tell Floyd the full details, as it was embarrassing, "Just a bit".

Loster moaned as he looked down to the river, "Brauhh". I wasn't sure if he was saying Bah or Bra? But my best guess was kinda both.

The boat kept us afloat, but we noticed the boat was acting strange like no other boat did. It obeyed his command. He wasn't really showing the way, but the boat showed him the way to go.

Grad sat down with us as Floyd asked, "What kind of boat do you use?"

"Oh, she's a special one I tell ya" he replied.

"But the way it hears your command", Floyd said, fascinated, "I haven't seen or heard a boat that does that. Why?"

"Bahhhh!" said Loster.

Grad nodded his head to the goat figure, "The boat has a mind of its own".

Floyd stared back, "Ah, right".

Of course, it did, but it didn't mean it would disagree with him or what. What boat does that? I mean, a boat with a mind of its own?

Then the boat moved and pushed me forward on the boat's floor, like it meant it.

"Are you okay?" Floyd asked me.

I grumbled, "Yeah, I have a thing with boats".

9) Fear of not being totally cool

We came into a slop in the river; it went on through a spooky tunnel where we were heading. It didn't exactly help us to see where it was leading.

We came towards another stone dock, where lay a tall iron door that gave you a shaky feeling. It was pretty dark, with no lantern to give anyone information about this area.

Loster was moaning and putting his head underneath the boat, while Floyd was shivering his teeth.

I glared at Floyd, "Anything the matter?" I asked him meanly.

He looked at me and put his hand on the goat's head. "No", he said charmingly, "I'm totally OK".

Loster held his head toward Floyd, and he jumped. I laughed out loud; it could have been called a swarm of whatever Floyd had called these creatures.

We landed on the dock as our new friend (I guess?) Grad, gave us one last favour. He gave me a small key that I almost thought was a tablet.

"It will help you get inside the treasure room," Grad said, and pointed at the door. I noticed there was a bit of ground that seemed to be dead.

"Are you sure you're not coming along?" I asked him.

"Nah," he responded, "I'll meet you outside. Besides, somebody has to look after this guy".

It was true, Loster didn't want to get out of the boat, even though he could get out if he wanted to. The goat was quite pale; maybe he just wanted to wish his friends farewell to their deaths.

Me and Floyd nodded at both of them, and we turned around and walked towards the door.

We stood there for a moment to figure out how to open it. "How do we open it?" I asked Floyd.

Floyd looked around on one side and pushed the door hard. It slowly opened and I opened the door on the other side.

It was very heavy as we pushed; it didn't help us much as we pulled with our muscles. I couldn't believe

Skull-Hat head and Goat-Dude couldn't help at least once in their lives.

When we managed to open the door, the problem was we had to act quickly. We got inside fast as it closed because these doors wouldn't stay open.

The tunnels were like a whole circle with tiny holes; I didn't want to ask what was inside them. We could have taken different paths, but it would have taken us forever to reach our destination.

Man, I was afraid to ask Floyd what these Spin-Cans really were. He was holding onto my phone as a light illuminator.

He felt more curious going forward than the spark of fear inside him. That is what I totally felt too.

"Do you have any experience with whatever they are?" I asked Floyd.

"What?"

"You know," I said, not trying to pop, "those Spin-Cans you and everyone are scared of".

He turned to look at me. "Listen, they are an extreme menace! They will climb over you till they stop having fun and set their fangs you wish you didn't see; they would kill a population you never knew about because they killed them in a week!"

Floyd seemed pretty tense; I never saw this side of him before, which meant this was much worse than I bargained for.

"If you say this is just a small thing, well, we've got more trouble on our hands!"

"Right, right", Floyd commented as he kept his mind in focus.

We walked further into the tunnel and left talking till later. I noticed there were scratches of drawings on the walls, and it looked pretty old - too old, in fact.

I did also notice we were getting into some green webs of sorts; bits of it were falling on the floor and turning into something else we were walking on. Something soft and sticky.

"Floyd?" I asked in disgust.

"Keep moving," he said, not turning back, "if you hear chips crack, don't turn around; if you see eyes coming around you, also: don't turn around; if you see a best friend who looked pretty cool and says he is, forget about him".

I didn't argue; I listened to Floyd's instructions as we kept at a fast pace.

We were walking faster; I wasn't sure why, but I noticed sounds were creeping along with us.

I also noticed that a few things might have passed by me. I know Floyd told me to NOT turn around, but when I did, I couldn't see what it was.

"You said not to turn around, but I did, and nothing showed up," I told Floyd. "What do you say will happen now?"

"I say you're dead," Floyd noted as if it was true, "but if you're here, then don't worry about it".

We came to a halt; we saw more drawings and many sticky webs that were in our way. But that wasn't why Floyd stopped.

He was white as a pea. He froze, paralysed; his face was as frightened as if he had seen the most horrible movie ever written, that made him cry and laugh simultaneously.

I turned around and looked right at him, "Hey, hey", I said to him calmly, "what's up?"

His face was still full of terror, "Ddddddd…".

"…what?" I asked, as I forgot something he said.

"Don't turn around," he said quietly and panicked, "Don't turn around!"

I did as I forgot immediately. Sorry, we are only human!

What I saw was a four-legged bug with a head of an ordinary person with big black eyes and fearsome teeth. He was the size of a puppy.

As terrified as I was, the only words I could say were, "He is ugly, isn't he?"

He roared as I squeezed quickly. "RUN!!!" Floyd screamed, and we ran pass it. We went where we came from and took different turns the wrong way. I didn't blame him. But the thing we just saw was coming after us, very fast!

We were stepping through webs on our clothes as we tried to take new routes, and the creature lurked on the walls.

When we ran through the tunnels, we saw others like him passing by on the ceiling in other tunnels as they screamed at us.

We turned into many other tunnels, but they led us to a nest of Spin-Cans that were alive!

We noticed the ones chasing us were on our tail, so we just marched forwards and interrupted the other ones from their sleep.

We were running with no stop; we noticed more of them coming to the other side and the ones behind us.

"Where do we go?" I yelled at Floyd as we kept running and took turns.

"Where to go, where to go?" he told to himself, worrying, "Oh! I know!"

He tossed me over to one small tunnel gap and flew himself next to me. We ducked our heads and saw the Spin-Cans flying by above us like a plague that wanted to pump somebody off a building.

I put my head right into the green ground. I wasn't ready to look. I wasn't ready to die by a Spin-Can.

It took a few minutes till Floyd leaned up and took a look. He looked at me and asked, "Are you OK?"

I didn't feel like putting my head up, not yet. "What do you think, mister Royal Robe man?"

He gave me an unsettling look, "Look, they will be coming for us very soon. We have to move now".

"No".

"OK, don't mind if I join you," he said as he pulled his arms across. I know he didn't want that, he was trying to be kind, but I know he really wanted to get out of there alive.

I look at him with one eye. I decided I should help this poor old fool out. I got up and looked down at him, "Come on", I called, "we need to find the Silver Rose, right?".

"Yes", he replied.

He got up, and we took off running. We knew and heard these things were still there; we just hoped we don't encounter them again.

10) Junkyard of Treasures

With so many scary encounters and challenging trails, we made it to the door. It was like the one we entered but smaller. Me and Floyd were a mess from our adventure, and we thought we should get this over with.

We just leant over to the door after running for our lives, and we were breathing profoundly and gasping.

"We just get the key in?" I asked Floyd.

"Yeah," Floyd replied, "it's in your pocket".

I took it out and kneeled over to the keyhole. The key was a small diamond that would open the door.

I saw a hole that looked like the same size as the key. I couldn't put it in as it didn't work like that.

"What are you waiting for?" Floyd asked, tedious.

"I can't get it in".

"You don't put it in; you put it inside".

I stared at him, "Wouldn't it get stuck, and we would get eaten?"

Floyd didn't say anything else; I listened to his advice. I put the thing in like a coin inside a machine.

Then I heard a rattling noise as the door opened. I looked at Floyd with a cheerful smile, "It's opening!"

"Told you it would".

We stepped away from the door. And what we saw was a storm of hills of lost treasures. Or another term I would have used: junk.

It wasn't as stunning as it was believed to be. It was OK, with stuff anyone wanted but lost. I heard the Gatekeeper say many of these things didn't belong here but came from different parts of the galaxy.

If that was the case; why were they here then? The Bark was a massive world that was full of many weird things. Sure, the gravel could've brought them through, but how far did it reach?

"So…this is it?" I said, disappointed.

"Yep," Floyd said with grudges, "What you think?"

"I was hoping for a shiny area where the rose might grow".

Floyd looked offended, "This is where the biggest treasure of all time is. This is some of their lost stuff, and that is all you got to say?"

I tried to think of something to win Floyd's support back, "…sorry?"

Floyd let it go as we started exploring, "So how can we find it?" I asked, "It's so big and is a mess".

"It won't be that hard," he said confidently; our amulets started to glow green. They were glowing faintly, so we knew for one thing:

"We're getting close," I said.

"It must be somewhere on the top pile", Floyd suggested, "it's where all the recent stuff came in".

"Well, I hope it is alright," I said, hoping.

It wasn't that difficult to locate where the Rose was, but it took Floyd and me a bunch of time digging over pile over pile of treasure to get to it.

I tried to look out for any dangerous objects that Floyd was throwing away. I wanted to remind him that whatever he was throwing shouldn't target me.

I mean, the place looked bad enough, but it didn't mean we should make more of an untidy mess.

"Does anyone come here?" I asked Floyd, "I mean, nobody wanted to check all this out and steal them for themselves?"

"You tell them about the Spin-Cans," he said, as it would be doubtful.

"Sure" I got the picture.

No wonder they can't get in here. Again, if they did know how to explore the entire world, they would not risk their lives to come in here and rob everything and get killed by hundreds of angry, hungry creatures that would eat every bone out of you.

I looked down at Floyd, who dug a hole in the pile. I was afraid to look at him because I thought he would fall inside it.

His amulet and mine were glowing heavily; they got so green we could tell we were close.

He was trying to rub the stuff still blocking him from reaching it. "We need to go deep", he stared at me to say something. "Get something that would pick up a load of this junk".

I nodded. I walked over to the ground and looked at what was close to me. I saw some stuff here that could come in handy: a massive space gun, big robot claws, a bomb (wait, what? Oh, it was a spaceship).

I picked up an excellent handy tool that might help us. I gave Floyd a tool I never thought I would carry. "Here," I called to him and passed him the small device.

He stared at it, "A grenade?"

"Yes!"

"You sure this is wise?"

"Well, it can't be that bad," I said, not thinking straight, but Floyd hit a button he didn't know about.

"What did you do?!" I told him that it was his fault.

"I didn't press a thing!" he said, freaking out, "What should we do?!"

I tossed the thing on the pile, and he ran down.

"No!!!" he screamed, "that's where the rose is!!!"

"It will be fine!!!" I said as we ducked for cover. Then a big red explosion blasted the treasure, and what remained flew above us.

We put our heads up and saw a lesser mess that seemed to be stomped on.

We smiled and rushed towards the area. But we came to a halt; something was wrong.

I stared at my amulet, and the green light was dimming. "Oh no", I called.

Floyd went over before me and saw something, "Blast!"

"What?" I ask, worrying, "what's wrong?"

I came over as his face was sinking. What was left of the rose was shiny pieces of glass that would have assembled a beautiful piece of art.

"Noononnono!" he said in nonsense.

We glared at the thing, and then I came back to Floyd, "Maybe we could take the remaining pieces to the Admiral!" I said hopelessly. "He would be fine about that, right?"

Floyd gave me a face that gave me worse news that I wasn't ready to face.

"No, he wouldn't!" Floyd said in hopelessness and worry. "He tried to get his hand on this to give to his wife! The one he loves, and now it's gone, and I'm going to lose my head for this!"

11) We Get Bad News

We were walking back to the Treasure Room entrance near the tunnel of the Spin-Cans, afraid and worried about what we were going to do.

The rose was destroyed, and Floyd told me everything was not going to be fine, so this had got us into more of a struggle than finding it.

But it happened; we came to a halt and got a call from the last person we wanted to talk to.

"Oh no," Floyd said, scared of the device that was ringing.

"Could you call him later?" I asked him quietly. We knew if we responded and told Admiral Keeill of what happened, he would definitely kill us.

Floyd turned his head to me, "I can't", he replied, like he had little choice, "He is a rich and reckless commander; if I don't call him back, he'll still put a bounty on my head".

"Why your head?" I asked as if that was important.

"Well, he gave me the job; you just came for the ride. But if he knew you had something to do with it, you would be on the list too".

"Great," I said, thinking it couldn't get any worse.

It sounded like Floyd didn't want to be on his bad side, which, by the way Floyd described it to me, made me nervous.

Floyd held out the device and showed it on the wall, and we saw a halo circle image on the wall.

"Admiral Keeill", Floyd said nervously, "how are you going?"

"I had a pretty busy day, Floyd," he generally said, paying no attention to what we had done. "I had to send a load of men to a cargo crew to lend supplies".

"How is it going out there?" Keeill asked.

Me and Floyd grinned with our teeth as we admitted, "We…ah, well…see, we…broke it".

"WHAT!!!" Keeill roared as he stood up, "I've been travelling back to my home world, and I gave you the most important task in our relationship, and you broke it!"

"You see, we sent a grenade, and it blew up".

"Didn't you ever consider it was made of diamonds"?

Floyd's face froze for less than a second, "Whaaaaat?" and glips.

Admiral Keeill didn't have a good expression on his face, I could tell. He was mad at us for causing a big deal. Something neither me or Floyd could fix, and we were going to get paid for it.

"OK, this is what we're going to do", Keeill spoke up like it was something we weren't going to like. "I'm going to send my personal squad and take you, either dead or alive, and I will deal with what remains you have".

Floyd stuck up his thumbs and tried to make a smile, "Great", he said, frightened.

The halo image disappeared, and we just stood there in dread.

Then an idea struck me, "You know that device that took us off Earth and went to Keeill's ship?" I asked, "What if we could use that and get out of here?"

"We can't," Floyd said grimly, "it only transports to his ship".

"Dang," I said, running out of ideas. It looked like, despite all my ideas, we were stranded with no options, and whenever the squad arrives, there was so little time.

Then Floyd was taking off his amulet. "We can't wear these anymore. They would know where we are".

I took mine off, and we threw them on the ground. "We need to leave here".

Loster and Grad were waiting for us when we arrived back at the dock. The Goat seemed sick like the driver had taken him through a couple of rounds about the river.

"How did things go?" Grad asked.

Me and Floyd didn't say a word, or better not to.

"No?" he said dimly, "no finding? Oh, I tell ya, things couldn't be better here too. Say! What if I take you back?"

"Wonderful", I said when we were seated. Floyd
and I were quiet all the way as the boat headed back.

We had no better luck in the last few minutes.
We were beaten by fate, and it got to us.

We returned to the Gatekeeper's house, and I was
out of my limits. Floyd stood at the stairs with doubts
and no plan to escape this mess.

I was in the lounge room with Grad, who was
still with us. What was his deal? Why was he always
there when we needed his help? He was like a cat who
helped his owner if the owner didn't know the cat was
there at all because it wasn't his.

"I saw things like this before," he said, trying to
make me feel better, which did little. "Me and my gang
wanted to hold a hand and help someone, but it would
seem fate took them".

"Are you here to talk about my origin story?" I
asked him, thinking this wasn't the time.

How could I? It was a pointless adventure where we ended up at a dead wall and should've been eaten by the Spin-Cans.

The guy kept silent for a moment. "But we lost each side of ourselves" he kept going, "we weren't sure if we would meet again or find any sign where the others went. But we knew we could keep going if we had to face our fate".

What he was saying kinda made sense. Maybe we didn't have to face our fate. Maybe we could still change it.

"Anyway, I don't see what's the point; you know what I mean?" Grad said. "You all go chase a rose that doesn't belong here. You and your friend go all around the Bark as you weren't sure where to go. I've heard of another like it…".

Then it struck me, "Wait, what did you say?!"

"I've heard of another like it" he replied, and his face told me he wasn't trying to make me a fool again. "The way everyone told me about it. I heard this somewhere else".

"Yes, but Grad. Do you know anything about a diamond rose?"

"A diamond rose?" he said in surprise. "Well, there was another rose; it's close. It had a familiar style like the one you were looking for. I think one of the boys knows its whereabouts".

I hugged the guy, "Grad, you're a lifesaver!" and I walked over to Floyd and told him all about it.

He stared at us and wondered, "You're sure?" Grad nodded.

"Floyd, what do you think this all means?" I asked him as if there was a glimmer of hope.

Floyd stared in deep thought, "If Grad is saying all these facts add up, it means we still have time".

We walked down the stairs to where the gang's basement was. Grad said this was a place where folks like himself and others go to chill out. It was mostly a hangout place.

"You're sure about this?" I asked Grad.

"Yes", he said confidently, "these guys know how to get around the Bark, and if they do, we do too!"

I had a small feeling about that sentence that he looked like an expert but what he said may not be as true as what he thought.

When we opened the door, it looked like a bar club with guys wrestling and singing along. Old-fashioned furniture decorated the club, a jukebox played music, and for some strange reason, a massive window gazed with no light on the other side. Seemed very cosy, I thought.

I looked at Grad, "What is this?"

"This is it! the Ba-gooey!" Gard said like this was paradise.

"But you said someone knows about the Sliver Rose replica?"

"Did somebody say replica?" said a firmer voice. We turned and walked up to a man sitting on an old-fashioned writer's chair who was looking out the window.

It was the Gatekeeper, sitting back as he fit in with all the others. He was holding a violin while playing it.

"You?!" Floyd asked, surprised. I didn't blame him; I felt the unexpectedness which I didn't predict.

"Doesn't anybody belong anywhere?" he said as if he thought he had seen the last of us.

"I'm quite surprised to see you here", I told him.

The Gatekeeper stared at me through his sunglasses as he decided to not take them off, "I go where I feel like it".

"He comes whenever he wants to", Grad explained joyfully, "he has the spirit of a chill bunny not running about the place".

"Thank you", the Gatekeeper told him very dishonestly.

"You know the other rose?" I asked him.

"I know it?" he said if I asked a stupid question, "I owned it, then gave it away".

"What?!" Floyd said in shock.

"Gatekeeper person," I told him. "We need it very desperately, like now".

"Who did you give it to?" Floyd asked urgently.

The Gatekeeper kept to his silence as he played a tune on his violin. He started to play it while we watched him. It looked like he didn't really care, or maybe he did; I could not tell with this guy.

"You sure look like you're in a hurry," he said.

"Well, that's the thing," Floyd said, not giving out our full story.

"This is the second time you have asked me to help you, TWICE!" he said very perfectly, "and that's only today. I think something is going on with you two".

"That's mostly our business, really," I said.

The Gatekeeper leaned forward and got up from his convertible seat as he sighed and decided to help us, "I gave it to mother nature itself, inside the Tree Link, a few docks and floors away".

"Ahh", Floyd moaned, "it would take us a while to get there if I would guess".

"Not likely," said Grad with a plan.

12) The Boat isn't Responding

We journeyed through steep and deep rivers that took us into wild splashes, where we thought we could have fallen into the water.

The boat sped up quickly as we were diving down steep tunnels and across rocks blocking our paths. We banged and clashed with them as we tried to hold on.

It was the most extreme and exciting ride I have ever been on, but Floyd was pretty terrified as he thought we might die.

It took us close to an hour to reach the Tree Link. Or the core of the Bark. It was said in legend that this was the heart of the world, a seed of the System of Trees, one of its children. Even though the story was bizarre, I couldn't imagine that I would ever encounter Mother Nature itself.

Me and Floyd had to hold on to the boat as Grad knew how to steer. "Are you trying to get us killed?!" I yelled at the boat.

"I wouldn't say that", Grad warned me.

"Why?" I said back.

"It has a mind of its own".

"I don't care!"

"Maybe you should listen to the driver" Floyd tried to calm me down, but he was trying to brace himself for another splash.

"Well, I don't care! This boat doesn't like me, and who cares, boat! Nobody likes you because you want them to not like you! You should take a swim!"

The boat started to creak deep, as I felt like the boat was overloaded.

"Oh no," Grad worried as he paid close attention to that sound, "but we're nearly there".

I wasn't sure what the boat was going to do. I knew it wasn't going to explode because it would kill itself while having its revenge. But it rocked heavily in the swift water from left to right, still going down in the steep river.

"No! No! No!" Floyd panicked as he kept hitting from either side.

Grad came down to me, "Apologise! Quickly!"

"No!" I said honestly as I had enough, "I'm not taking another trip with this…" it rolled again to shut me up. It was tilting itself as I and the others held on the boat's edge. "OK! OK," I said, "I'm sorry! I don't know why you keep acting like this and I'm trying to get used to…".

"It's not going to work," Gard said as if I blew that chance, "we have to jump overboard!"

"Jump over what?" Floyd asked before we jumped off the boat, and the ship turned upside down as it went down.

We had to swim our way to the Tree Link as our boat decided to drop into the river.

We were stinking wet as we came over to shore. We went to a soft ground leading us towards another tunnel with vines showing us the way.

I was gasping from the water out of my mouth, and the only words I could say was, "The Boat destroyed itself!"

"It doesn't do that", Grad said, surprised, "well…not most of them".

"I'm sorry!" I could only say, "That boat wasn't going to put up with our nonsense. It wanted to do it whenever I stepped onboard".

I looked at Floyd with aggressive looks, "You see what she did, Floyd!"

"Well, I saw a bit," he said honestly, trying to understand what happened.

I dropped my jaw as I couldn't be in more shock than I was right now. Whatever that boat's life was, she might have done us a massive favour.

But that wasn't our concern anymore; we had to make our way over to the tunnel and find that rose. But I could tell we were expected.

When we walked further inside the tunnel, it was getting lighter, like the sun had a turn-on button. I couldn't tell what we were stepping into, but we seemed to expect something to show up.

We arrived in a room full of vines all over the place, and there was nothing but some creepy plants.

"Huh, this isn't the place", Floyd considered.

"But this has to be", I thought, looking everywhere I could see, "there's plants! There's…there's mother nature stuff".

Even though I wanted to be very self-confident, Floyd was right. I could see nothing in this sizeable wide area, nothing at all.

But what we missed was a plant that formed out like a flower and transformed into a grass woman with nature clothing, like a dress with big eyes and flower hair.

We turned in surprise, "Ookay..." I said, surprised by the experience.

"Welcome, visitors", she greeted us.

"uhhh…hi", spoke Grad as he kneeled.

She glared at us as if we were being expected as human beings. "You look like you travelled from places across the stars".

"Uh, yeah, I guess so" Floyd replied, thinking she read our minds.

"We are the Guardians of the Bark", she said as if we should know what that was. "There aren't many of us anymore; most are extinct or have evolved into something greater".

"Like what?" I asked, then I recalled, "The trees?" It was kinda obvious if I thought of it more clearly.

She held her hand over to one of the vines. She turned it into piles of grown roses and flowers, and the room felt very bright and wonderful.

"The flowers call for themselves to be born; I gave them gratitude and purpose on being on these worlds. There haven't been Guardians like me on every world because they can't keep growing".

Then She looked at me, "But I can. Welcome everyone to the Planet of the Trees!"

It seemed wild, but I wasn't sure how to move along with that speech.

"Yes, do you recall the origin of this planet?" Floyd asked.

"It was split from our galaxy's tree. It was cut, and pieces were scattered across the galaxies to make a new home for many new worlds".

"So, what you're saying right now, all this, is the origin of the trees?" I asked in shock.

With a very unexpected revelation that I picked out, she responded, "Yes!" so epically, I couldn't put my mouth into words.

"Wow!" I said.

"Wow!" Floyd said.

"Hmm," Grad didn't mind it.

"The Tree has been living for so long now," she said, "its growth couldn't end; even when one root is torn, another is grown".

"So it repeats," I guessed, "over and over again".

"Yes, but nothing would change it. Our system has been built, and it couldn't be destroyed. It can't be, even if you seek to destroy life".

"Miss," I told her, "we need to find a rose if you don't mind lending it to us?"

She gasped out loud with a shocked expression, and her flowers in the room screamed like tiny insects.

"You dare try to steal one of our precious children?" she spoke, horrified.

"Well, it was given to you; it's not yours…" Floyd tried to be reasonable, which was getting worse.

"If you knew anything about our nature! We shall take things that matter to you!" she said very threateningly, which I wouldn't dare to challenge her.

She was mad at us, I could tell. We were getting something maybe worse. Other flowers that folded up and came out were plant monsters with flower heads and nasty teeth. Their bodies were made of vines, and they had long finger claws.

Floyd pointed to them, "Now that's why I say Nature is evil".

If we wanted to get out, we couldn't. The beasts were surrounding us as we tried to look for a way out.

I could see a small gap through a wall that we could get to. I took Floyd's hand, and we ran right through it. The monsters tried to scratch us, but we luckily escaped.

But we forgot Grad. "Don't worry, guys! I'll find my way home!" he said as he ran back to the surface.

Me and Floyd had double trouble on our hands! An angry Admiral that we broke his wife's wedding gift, and an angry Mother Nature we were robbing something that wasn't hers. What had I got myself into?!

13) When Things Get Big

We came into a massive forest environment that shined our way, with giant trees reaching towards a roof that seemed like the sky, but I knew it wasn't. It was amazing. Me and Floyd glared for a bit, but we knew we weren't safe.

We still had plant monsters chasing after us, and it wouldn't take them long till they reached us. "Where should we go?" I asked Floyd.

Weird bird and monkey sounds were heard around us above the trees. "Ah, that way", Floyd suggested, and we moved on. Wherever we went, the noises followed us.

We were in a jungle with so much green; it was nature at its tidiest, with grass on the ground everywhere. Vines were pulling down in front of us, blocking our way. I thought I had had enough of nature, but nature had a purpose for us.

I just hoped next time when I go to my brother's wife's garden, the plants wouldn't try to eat me.

Vines from the trees were trying to grab us. We didn't have a sword to chop them away, so, bad news - we had to run for it!

We had to keep running. I never knew running was so good.

Then we froze. We saw some of the plant monsters around the place. They glared at us with their fearsome teeth.

"Like, dude! Don't these guys clean their teeth?" I asked Floyd.

"Well, that's their specialty," Floyd replied.

"What?"

"Flowers?" he took my hand, and we ran.

We had to dodge trees, vines and the monsters. They weren't moving fast, and thankfully they were no Spin-Cans. But they would eat us, nonetheless.

When I was running, I thought if there was some other way we could do it, there had to be some way to get Plant Woman to help us out. We had so much on our plates as it was.

Soon the monsters tried to grab me. It wasn't fun, I say. We were running out of places to go; we couldn't shake them if we kept going through the trees. It would not make things any different.

I noticed a tree was about to collapse on Floyd as I acted; I pushed him over on the other side as we landed on the ground.

I looked at him as we groaned, "You okay?"

"Not the right word I would use", he said.

We noticed behind us a few of the plant monsters were searching for us. We crept over to a log as we tried to keep quiet.

Floyd gave me a gesture as we should move slowly and not alert them. We stood up and took one step at a time.

Then another plant monster jumped from a tree near us as I squill. Floyd took my hand as we run, while a pack of them followed our trail.

We came for a short pause as we saw more of these things were rising from the ground, as grasses of their bodies bound together.

We made a shift turn as we have to avoid them. Me and Floyd had a worrying feeling that these guys were spawning wherever we go, and we might be giving out their seeds.

I spotted more emerging everywhere I looked. It made me very scared, as I didn't know if we would ever get out of this.

We were too surrounded and had no idea where to go. We would be dead soon, I could tell, but I wasn't wishing for it.

Then we spotted a cliff dead ahead. There was no other way to turn. We had to make a jump.

We landed on the ground which was only ten feet down. We also noticed as we got up there was a field dead ahead. We kept running as we hadn't encountered any other danger.

We came to a stumble and tripped over the field of grass. We were dead, that's all I could say. But something was glowing right ahead of us.

We put our heads up and saw another Silver Rose. It was glamming in beauty. I mean, wow, it looked cool. It was shaped like a rose, a circle with wonder and its leaves poking out.

The Woman was there walking to it.

"Please!" I tried to reason with her, "just give it to us!"

The grass was shaped of vines around our hands and feet, trying to trap us.

"You know you can't escape Nature, not while you commit the crime you committed," She said.

"See?", Floyd told me unimpressed, "they don't seem to understand common sense".

I squirrel by the grass that was tight by my hands and feet. I had to reason with her. It was the best I could do.

"Listen!", I called out, "you must understand, that isn't a normal rose! Its not even from the System of Trees! We really need it for great importance!"

When she did look at the Rose, she was surprised and quite unaware of it, "this…this is a different kind I have never seen before".

She reached over to the shiny Rose with her hand. She started to glow without realizing it.

The plant monsters were behind us, in huge numbers, I couldn't tell how many.

I didn't know what was happening to her, but I had to stop her!

"Listen! Step away…" I called out.

But what happened was this: she faded and turned into a giant grass that scrolled up into the Bark and reached into the roof. The monsters stopped and watched and then ran away.

I couldn't tell what was happening; it was like an earthquake, and the jungle was trembling.

Our hands and feet were freed, and I went over to Floyd, "We have to get out!"

"Agreed!" he said, as we went over and saw the Silver Rose. Floyd pulled it off the ground as we took off.

It wasn't good; the place was falling apart. Branches fell over us, and the grass was waving like it needed to be saved.

There was nothing we could do but let Mother Nature do Her thing.

14) The Conversation

Good News: whatever happened back in the Jungle didn't harm anything in the Bark. Bad News: we had some word from Marshall and Grad's pals that Admiral Keeill's men had arrived.

At least we had a Silver Rose that was close enough to what Admiral Keeill wanted. It wasn't the exact same thing he wanted, but it was 91% to the likeness.

We waited at The Gatekeeper's house again. Grad, Marshall and the Gatekeeper sat around with us in the lounge room, with sleepy goat sitting next to their mammoth.

We all stared at the Rose, not only in amazement that we found something so identical to it, but we had to come up with a plan and fast.

"You're sure that's them?" Floyd asked.

"They're sure", Grad replied, "men wearing shady grey armour with Red goggles in their helmets".

"Gosh, that's them", Floyd replied, knowing our time was up.

"Then we have to have a plan," I said, holding the Rose. "Could we try to give them the Rose and explain about it and get it over with?"

"Yeah, but we can't contact Keeill", Floyd explained. "We destroyed the amulets that allowed us to talk to him, and we are out of reach. We're no good as dead".

The odds weren't looking good. It was a bit impossible to share contact with somebody who wanted to hunt you down, and with all the challenges we had been through in the Bark, I didn't want to go through all that again.

And with Keeill's Squad all over the place searching for us, it would be even more impossible.

While we tried to figure out the right plan, I had an awful plan which I disagreed with as quickly as possible. But as I rethought any other ideas: this had to be the one.

"Then we'll meet him upwards," I said as everyone looked at me. Everyone had an impression that my idea wasn't very reliable.

"You think that's a good plan?" Marshall asked.

"We've been through worse," I said, relaxed. I looked at Floyd, "You think he'll be up at the gravel?"

"Could be?" Floyd wondered if it could be possible.

I turned to Grad, who I thought was some fool first, but was a big help to us. I don't think me and Floyd could manage everything without him. The least I could do is to ask him for one last favour, "Grad, you may know your way up there?"

"That I do," he said.

"Excellent!"

"Hold on", the Gatekeeper stopped us, "if you're going with this, you could be dead anyway".

"We'll just have to trust our guts on this one," I said as we wished our friends goodbye, and they promised they wouldn't tell anyone where we were going.

We walked through the streets once again. Folks were getting more crowded than usual. I wasn't sure what the meaning was, but it just was.

Then I noticed men in armour searching the street. I turned around as Floyd and Grad stopped.

"What's the matter?" Floyd asked.

My eye turned in their direction, "They're here".

"Oh boy," Floyd called, scared.

We turned towards a small alleyway. We saw them only two walks away asking the aliens about us. They stood there for several minutes as folks informed them about every detail. We could tell we weren't going anywhere.

"I'll distract them," Grad told us he was going to take that chance.

"But they'll kill you," I told him to do no more stunts. I had enough of what he did; the last thing I wanted from him was to die properly.

"Well, at least I could die, right?" he said, trying to make a bad joke. "When I run, go forward to the next turn after the two lefts, go straight and turn left, and then go right; there you shall find an odd door where there is a hidden corridor, and it will lead you to another elevator".

I was so glad he did something so incredibly encouraging on our adventure; I was sad that he was doing this heroic thing. The only thing I could do was look right at him and say, "Thank you for everything you did".

He nodded and made contact with my eyes, a cheeky and happy glare. He ran out and called the troopers, "Hey! You want information? Come and get me!"

The troopers chased him, and we left our post.

We took the elevator we found just as Grad told us. It took us all the way to the top, and we arrived at the same open gravel. It was still empty like before, but with just the random elevator.

I stepped out and tried not to sink. Floyd learnt from the mistake I made and didn't act a fool like myself.

I noticed that as we walked further in the distance, the elevator went back down, and we saw no more sign of it. We were on our own one last time.

"Where should we find them?" I asked Floyd.

Floyd had no idea where they would be. However, he gave me a very confident look.

We soon found a spaceship in the sky passing by. It looked like a red rocket but upgraded a bit with cooler detail.

It landed down, and we knew they had found us. Instead of getting out, they beamed out with big guns aimed at us.

"Floyd and friend!" said the one in charge, "you're coming with us! Either dead or alive!"

"Yes, thank you!" Floyd called out from a distance, "we have a deal to make!"

"There will be no more games here, Mr Floyd! Just surrender, and we'll get this over with".

It sounded like there wouldn't be any options here, which was a real shame on our behaviour.

Floyd paused as he took one step, but I had a funny feeling. I stopped in Floyd's tracks. "What are you doing?" he told me.

I eyed him, trying to warn him, "This could be a trick".

"A trick?!" he asked.

"Move away, Miss!" said the commander.

I knew that wherever there was a solider in high command, you should follow his order, but I knew if we do this, we were better dead than to go with them.

I stood with Floyd, trying to be brave and confident with my friend. "No", I called out.

"We shall fire at you two", he warned, "there will be no other option".

"What if we did what they say to do?" Floyd whispered to me.

"We're not having this," I told him to be quiet. I felt pretty strong about this, taking our stand on what to do - which was a bad move. Oops!

"Five!" the commander called.

"I mean, I don't want to die. Not even today".

"Floyd," I said confidently, "we don't really get a vote in this".

"Four!"

"Let's say they did take us; what happens next?"

"Three!"

"Then Keeill will think we were lying since we had another Rose. He'll put us in a space jail?"

"Two!"

We were running out of time. Floyd had to make a decision right now, in fact! He wasn't sure what to do. He only came with one option.

He jumped over to the soldiers, and they stunned both him and me. We dropped on the gravel (not sinking, thank goodness) and we got rather nauseated.

The soldiers came over to us and took us with them. Who knew what might happen next, but this could change the course of our story…

15) The Conclusion to Our Story

Our heads were dazzling when we passed out; we couldn't focus on our vision as everything was blurry and dazzling. We also couldn't think as our minds weren't active.

It was a few hours after we were shot, and we thought that was it. But I wish we were still passed out because I didn't want to be in space prison. I mean, I had a life!

When I woke up and saw my vision cleared, we were back at Keeill's table. We were sitting back at the exact same spot as before.

Bodyguards were outside if we did anything hasty, and Keeill was not in a good mood.

"So, what now?" he asked as if he was giving us one last chance. I was hopeful if that was the case.

"Mr, Admiral, Commander, sir!" Floyd said on his feet, "we can definitely explain!"

"No!" Kill interrupted, "I gave you this task, and you broke our agreement".

"I think we can go further than explaining," I said, trying not to torment Floyd.

"Yes indeed", Keeill agreed with me.

"What?" Floyd said in confusion, "I mean…it wasn't an easy job to do".

"And look where that got you?" Keeill spoke again.

Floyd pleaded to Keeill, "OK, we had another plan, and I hope this would work for both you and your wife".

Floyd passed over the Silver Rose to Keeill. "This is a replica of the original, but I hope this would work finely as well. Please, sir, don't execute me or my friend for this extremely difficult, terrifying, painful trip".

Keeill glared at it with a smile. He took a more extended look to take in the full detail of the art. It wasn't quite the same, but he was pleased, nevertheless. "Well, I could tell my wife I found a more advanced sculpture of the rose?"

"I think that's a great idea, Admiral," I told him.

"Then…you are free of your duties," Keeill said happily.

Floyd dropped in relief or confusion at what we said, "Th…wha…ha…", he could hardly speak.

"But Floyd", the Admiral told him, "if you ever wanted to take on another job, you know who to call".

He gave a blank and lost expression as his thoughts couldn't comprehend what was going on.

I walked over to him and whispered in his ear, "I'm just somebody who saved your life".

He squealed and said quietly, "Thhhhhank youuuuu".

Well, that was it. Well, at least I thought it was. But every journey has a destination, doesn't it?

We went back to the garden where I had been at my sister's wedding. I noticed it was the exact time we left. I think I also learnt about Time Travel.

I could still hear the wedding ceremony continuing as if I didn't miss much. I could hear people talking at the tables.

It seemed so bizarre that you have travelled millions of light years, meeting scary and incredible creatures and people, and then back to reality.

"Is that it?" I looked back at Floyd.

"Yep," he said, "Well, I'd better be going".

"Wait, wait, wait, wait," I told him quickly, "Are you really going to leave like that?"

He looked surprised and remembered I had a wedding to go to. "Oh!" he said, "sorry, I had so much going on I feel like I'm getting my head out of a jar".

"Come on," I told him, "I had to go on your bonkers adventures; you can come into one of mine".

Floyd turned his face away from me; I couldn't see what his face was saying. Maybe he thought he might not be fascinated, but he turned and said, "Well…why not" he said, not convincing.

When I took his arm, he smiled, and we walked out and headed towards the tables.

I soon stopped with Floyd to ask an important question, "Wait!"

"What?"

"Can I say that you're like my boyfriend?"

Floyd stared at me for some time and blanked out, "You are joking?"

THE END

Appendix: Liam the Author

This Appendix is included for those who are interested in how Liam became an author and how he develops his ideas. Liam hopes that this can create understanding that people with his disabilities can have great things to say and share with the world. Liam also hopes that all those who share his disabilities and want to write can hopefully benefit from learning about how he does it.

Liam starts with notes for a story, like the first example below. (Liam finds handwriting much more difficult than two-finger typing.) He then brainstorms an outline of ideas for the plot. As the outline example below shows, he often uses chapter headings to reflect the progress of the story up-front.

When he writes the actual story he just doesn't stop till its done, usually within a few weeks. When Liam started his business in August 2022, he had written the base stories of around 10 stories which he is gradually editing and printing. (Now he has added about four more).

After the base story is done, Liam takes his time to come back in to do edits of the story and try to improve his spelling and grammar as best he can. This can take quite a while. When he is happy with it, he hands on to his mum to edit for spelling and grammar that he has not been able to do.

His mum tries to keep Liam's own way with words as much as possible – hence the books are not like professionally edited books, and his mum is not perfect either! The books are the proud work of her son with disability, so she does not want to detract from the authenticity of that, while still making them readable to others. She then hands back to Liam so he can correct anything she has misunderstood. Sometimes they have discussions during editing to work out what Liam actually meant and how to best say it. When Liam is happy, his mum does a final read, correcting any outstanding errors she can find, and its ready for printing.

Before Liam could read and write, (which was not till late in his teen years), but as soon as he could hold a crayon, Liam was prolific with his storytelling using pictures. Generally, these were long comic-strip-type stories. An example of this is the final attachment. Liam has folders and folders of these picture stories.

Wedding or plon + book, Idunno,"

#1 Gurdening, welting, or,
Birth dys celbrating, + a wl is bums
ant, she Dsbided to plis hide &
seek with her noise.
Ishe tried to find her, a man sits
on a Branch as he wis reiding somekind
Si-Fi Novvel. She asK him wherc her
neisois, he point with his arm wide.
She wonder what he is reiding, he sais
her hand as it means everything an the lify
She asK him whshis hole as he wasnt
invited, he said he wis writing for something, he tells howrlinot life is so
unforsnont, as he wis about to lewe she
asks ilohz.
thes irrivean a space ship as theslea-
invited, thes wavn emilents siduil
thesive hecKs, this was a wetting
event ar whit, gon desity
later...

Floed shows her how telent he
is is he Disirevt a Guvd av Wnt.
"han bee?" he shows her ' how this!"
Disecvd, "\see? nowthis! soep', how,
this!"
"ok, I get it!" she said
Floht exidentls Dror fewof his
cavd,

. plinot Grivel
. soon thes Oo accaunter plinots

Original Outline for System of Trees

Below is Liam's original brainstorm/outline for System of Trees, written on 20 March 2021, which contains all major plot and character ideas.

SYSTEM OF TREES

I.	An Unwelcome Guest, or just another Stranger
II.	The Gift
III.	On Top of a Tree City
IV.	Unfimler Friends
V.	The planet of (????)
VI.	The Ruins of Rul'ah
VII.	Nobody asks a seaweed
VIII.	The Goat headed guy
IX.	Tunnels of Dead Vines
X.	A Junkful of No Goods
XI.	The Boat of Not Responding
XII.	A Secret of a Secret
XIII.	Plants agents Nature
XIV.	One Plan, or die anyway
XV.	The Barging

Act 1:

Charlette is just an ordinary girl who lives in a quiet life, but wanted to more in her life than what it is. She was attending her sister's wedding and wasn't enjoying herself.

Meanwhile, while playing hide and seek with her nese, she bumps into a complete stranger named Floyd. She thought he was the most perdicler person she ever met, when Floyd told her about some weird stuff, she wanted to come with him.

Plot Point 1:

When Floyd and Charlette arrive at Abbranail Keeill, he wanted to hire them to go and hunt down his wife's lost dimond ring that was lost in the system of trees. While Floyd resently hatting that kind of enviorment, Charlette helped him overcome the trails that awaits them.

Act 2:

On their difficult journey, they soon discover on where the Dimond is and found it.

Plot Point 2:

While founding the dimond, Floyd exadently broke it and had to call back to Abbranil Keeill who later was disrtot about the issue and wanted exacutsion for Floyd and Charlette.

Act 3:

While trying escaping, Abbrnail desided a barging for Floyd to make, if he'll give himself up, he would pay him six billon checks and keep Charlette as prisoner to their empire. But Charlette disimproves that.

Floyd and Charlette make place to stay cover and make a plan to stop Abbrnial Keeill's army.

Climax:

While being caught, Floyd and Charlette were given to Keeill's ship with no escape, but Floyd later assembled the dimond (well, one that's close like it). Keeill looked at it carefully and thought this is close enough as it could get.

Keeill let them go and wanted to give Charlette a wedding presdent for her sister as a repayment as she was the one who helped all the way.

Floyd dropped Charlette off to the park, but Charlette though for all the trouble and the adventure, she thought at least Floyd could stay at least. Floyd attendet and thought it wouldn't be that bad of an idea.

On their journey, Floyd and a Charlette go to the tree world to meet a somebody who knows where the Dimond is, but they meet LO-NO and YO-NO as they try to get Floyd back to his duites. But Floyd wanted to refuse and keep adventuring.

Some part in the story, LO-NO and YO-NO go to another planet: a more hot desret world where they thought Floyd might be at, but they get a singal that he is in the Break.

They soon meet a head goat man who lived in a unral house with stairs that would lead to different parts of the world.

He lived with also unrasual creatures like an owl head
guy who is muscler. He also helps them on their journey,
he also knows takes them on the boat. And the
Gatekepper: who has the locks on the doors throw the
world. He is an eldryman who wears sunglasses and
likes jazz.

"the Boat has a mind of it's own" said the goat figer.
Floyd stairs back, "ah, right".
Of course it does, it doesn't mean it would disagree with
him or what.

The main world of where the Dimond is inside of a
planet of wood and bark.
Inside the planet, there is a village of trees, a basement
of a man and his friends. There is a secret cave that no
body enters with no lights (with bug/spider creature that
lives inside), a room with random tressures. And a nature
area with grass and plants, lots of plants.

Gravel planet.

Example of Liam's unedited writing

A portion of Chapter IV is reproduced here in Liam's words written as best as he can, between 22 March 2021 and 18 October 2022, before his mum edits.

IV) Unfamiliar Friends

The first Woodling we integrated was one on a hill street, where we could see the horizon and the landing bay. He was outside a clubhouse with a sigh of weird langue that even Floyd tried to spell the atoldpet.

The weirdest thing was the guy was creaking. I mean, he wasn't talking but creaking. "what's wrong with him?" I ask Floyd.

He was listing very carefully to him as each creak passed. The worst thing about it was the wood guy made these horrifying expressions that scared me out.

"They don't really communicate than normal English" Floyd replied, "they speak only in a tone that, like animals, could only respond to".

"so, you're saying they're speaking in another langue we can't understand?" I asked.

"Precisely," he said as he kept listing to the creaking wooden man.

We stood there for another few seconds; what I only heard was creaking and also a similar creaking from before.

I had no clue if Floyd knew how to speak tree or what, but I'll say, is an excellent listener.

When the tree man stopped creaking, he turned around and left us. Floyd's eye towards me, "he said he knows a guy who knows the whereabouts of the Rose".

"Yes!" I said gladly. I don't know how he manages it, but I was relieved.

"but he said it's in another system".

"oh", I said not sure what to think.

The only problem that lay on my mind was home; what if I spent too long away from home? But again, we're just talking to wood people.

Before we kept going, we heard someone panic. We know already knew trees don't scream, and mostly everyone here is a tree.

Liam telling his stories through cartoons

(before he could use words well enough to write)

Liam drew pictures from an early age, setting out his stories in his comic form, often divided into chapters. He was prolific in his comic-story drawing all through his childhood. Below is one example of an 8-chapter story.

CHAPTER
3
CHAPTER
4
100

CHAPTER
5
CHAPTER
6
3:43

CHAPTER
7
CHAPTER